TAKEN

TAKEN

EDWARD BLOOR

Alfred A. Knopf

New York

THIS IS A BORZOI BOOK PUBLISHED BY ALFRED A. KNOPF

www.randomhouse.com/teens

Educators and librarians, for a variety of teaching tools, visit us at
www.randomhouse.com/teachers

The Library of Congress has cataloged the hardcover edition of this work as follows:
Bloor, Edward.
Taken / Edward Bloor.
p. cm.
SUMMARY: In 2036 kidnapping rich children has become an industry, but when thirteen-year-old Charity Meyers is taken and held for ransom, she soon discovers that this particular kidnapping is not what it seems.
ISBN 978-0-375-83636-7 (trade) — ISBN 978-0-375-93636-4 (lib. bdg.) —
ISBN 978-0-440-42128-3 (tr. pbk.) — ISBN 978-0-375-89075-8 (e-book)
[1. Kidnapping—Fiction. 2. Social classes—Fiction.
3. Gated communities—Fiction.] I. Title.
PZ7.B6236Tak 2007
[Fic]—dc22
2006035561

Printed in the United States of America

10 9 8 7

First Trade Paperback Edition

For Pam

Everybody knows the deal is rotten.
Old Black Joe's still pickin' cotton
For your ribbons and bows
And everybody knows.

—Leonard Cohen

Kidnapped

Once you've been taken, you usually have twenty-four hours left to live.

By my reckoning, that meant I had about twelve hours remaining.

The blue numerals on my vidscreen showed the time, 11:31, and the date, 01-01-36. From where I was lying, the blue glow of the vidscreen provided the only color in the room. If it was a room. Other than the screen, all I could see were white walls. All I could hear was a low thrumming, like an engine.

Ever since I'd come to my senses, though, I'd felt strangely calm. Not like a sedated calm, either, although I had definitely been sedated. No, it was more of a logical calm. I was trying not to panic; trying to think things through.

I was not in this room of my own free will. Therefore, I was a prisoner. Logically, then, I must have been "taken," the popular euphemism for "kidnapped."

If you lived in The Highlands, like I did, then you were an expert on kidnapping. I even wrote a paper on the subject. It was filed right there on my vidscreen, along with the other papers I had written last term: "The World Credit Crash," "Metric at Midnight, 2031," and "The Kidnapping Industry."

I tried to sit up, but I couldn't. I had a strap tied around my waist, holding me to the bed. Or was it a stretcher? Yes, I remembered. It was a stretcher.

I could move my arms, at least. I could reach over and press MENU. The screen was still active, but it looked like all input and output functions had been disabled. Not surprising, if I had been taken.

My own files, though, were still accessible to me. I located my recent term papers and clicked on the pertinent one. Here is part of what it said:

> The Kidnapping Industry, by Charity Meyers
> Mrs. Veck, Grades 7–8
> August 30, 2035
>
> Kidnapping has become a major growth industry. Like any industry, though, it is subject to the rules of the marketplace. Rule number one is that the industry must satisfy the needs of its customers. That is, if parents follow the instructions and deliver the currency to the kidnappers, the kidnappers must deliver the taken child back to the parents. If the

kidnappers do not fulfill their part of the bargain, then future parents will hear about it, and they will refuse to pay. The trust between the kidnappers and the parents will have broken down.

The kidnapping industry today in most areas of the United States usually operates on a twenty-four-hour cycle (although a twelve-hour cycle is not uncommon in areas outside of the United States). In the majority (85%) of cases, the parents deliver the currency and the kidnappers return the child within the twenty-four-hour period.

Kidnappers' demands usually include a warning to parents not to contact the authorities. It is hard to estimate, therefore, how many parents have actually received ransom instructions and obeyed them to the letter. Professional kidnappers always include a Plan B in their instructions, describing a second meeting place in case the first falls through. In a minority (12%) of cases, unprofessional crews have murdered their victims right away and continued the ransom process dishonestly.

Several related industries have emerged as a result of the rise in kidnappings. For example, special security companies now track victims who have not been returned but who are thought to be still alive. These companies can gain access to FBI data. Unlike the FBI, however, these companies are willing to search for taken children in unsecured areas of the United States and in foreign countries.

The paper went on from there to describe common after-effects on taken children and to cite many alarming statistics about kidnapping, supplied by the *stateofflorida.gov* and *TheHighlands.biz* content sites. Cases of *reported* kidnappings increased by 22 percent in the last three years. However, estimates are that *unreported* kidnappings increased as much as 800 percent in the same time period.

The statistics only reinforced what I already knew. It's what every kid knew: if kidnappers identify your parents as people with a lot of currency in their home vault—dollars, euros, pesos, yuan—then you are a target. And if you don't get returned right away, there's not much the authorities can do about it. They are only willing to track you so far. Even now, there are parts of Florida and Texas that are beyond the reach of regular police forces. And from there, who knows? The Caribbean, Mexico, South America? Once you are gone to one of those places, you stay gone.

The sedated feeling in my head was clearing, leaving a dull ache in my stomach and in the space behind my eyes. I was starting to remember things. I was starting to put the pieces together. The white metal walls and the thrumming engine sound made more sense. I remembered where I was: in an ambulance. That's how the kidnappers got past all the security at The Highlands. They showed up in an ambulance.

And the guards opened the gates.

Then Victoria and Albert opened the door.

Then—

Suddenly I heard voices just outside the ambulance, low, gruff voices. They were arguing in Spanish, I think. Or it might have been Creole. Both languages are common in Florida. They were the voices of the kidnappers, the phony ambulance doctors.

How could the security guards have been so stupid? How could Victoria and Albert have been fooled so easily? I knew as soon as I saw "Dr. M. Reyes" that something was wrong with him. He didn't look or act like a real doctor. And he didn't talk at all, not until we were in the ambulance, pulling away. Then he talked in the kind of low, gruff voice that I was hearing.

Dr. Reyes was giving orders outside the ambulance door, orders to the other kidnappers. How many were there?

His Spanish was too fast for me to understand. Was he talking about the ransom payoff? Had my father agreed to his terms? Was he planning on keeping his end of the bargain and returning me unharmed once he had the currency? That, of course, would be the best scenario for everybody. Killing me would be the worst—for his industry, for him, and, of course, for me.

Maybe he was talking about my GTD. Children in The Highlands and in other wealthy developments usually have GTDs—global tracking devices. These are tiny bio-med transmitters that are inserted somewhere in their bodies. They were marketed to parents as a way to keep track of a kid's whereabouts 24/7/52. GTDs were supposed to bring about the end of the kidnapping industry. Instead, they have introduced a grisly new stage into the process.

Some kidnappers use repurposed medical equipment—X-ray machines, magnetic scanners, et cetera—to try to locate the GTD in the kid's body. It may be in a tooth, under a toenail, in an earlobe. Then the kidnappers surgically remove that body part.

The GTD industry would prefer that its customers not know about that stage. They spend billions highlighting their successes on infomercials, showing happy kidnap victims reunited with happy parents while hangdog kidnappers look on in handcuffs. But they can't suppress the truth. My friend Patience has an older brother named Hopewell. He was taken three years ago, just before they moved to The Highlands. After delivery of a ransom, he was left along the side of a country road, holding a bloody bandage to the left side of his head.

The worst thing about those GTDs is that even the kids themselves don't know where they are located. If kids knew, I guess they would talk about it. So instead, kids go to the doctor's office, are given a light anesthetic, and wake up with a GTD in some mystery part of the body. Only the parents know where.

Since my father is a doctor, he had installed mine himself. He kept the GTD tracking device with him at all times. So did he know yet that I had been taken? He wasn't at home when it happened. Were the kidnappers able to contact him to get the twenty-four-hour clock running? Did they tell him that they would start amputating my body parts if he even thought about using the GTD tracker? Or was he too busy watching college football to even bother answering his vidphone?

And what about my stepmother, my ex-stepmother? She was not at home to receive instructions, either. Only Victoria was. What would she do? What would she advise my parents to do? Would they cooperate with the kidnappers exactly, to the letter? That's what the FBI, the Highlands security staff, and the police advise.

I had to believe they would cooperate. They would read the instructions carefully; they would put the currency in a bag; they would drop it off where they were told to. That's what *I* would do, and I counted on them to do it, too. Right. That's what would happen. There was no reason to worry myself into a mental state.

I looked again at my vidscreen, sensing that something was different, and I was right. The camera light was on! The red laser at the top center was trained right on me while some creep was watching me on a monitor. Who was it? Where was he? I felt a flash of anger. But then I started to feel a sense of panic bubbling up in my throat like a series of wet, disgusting burps. Some stranger, some criminal, was watching me!

I tried not to move. I tried not to show any emotion in case they were transmitting this scene back to Victoria. I didn't want her to see me panicking and crying and hysterical. I could *acquit* myself (a Mrs. Veck word) better than that, I hoped. I had been trained well in how to behave at a moment like this.

Or had I?

Why was my throat constricting like it was trying to choke me? Why was the blood pounding so loud in my ears that I wanted to scream?

To shut down the rising panic in my head, I concentrated, hard, on my surroundings, on the four walls around me. The door to the ambulance was there beyond my feet, just one meter away from the foot of the stretcher. That meant that the front cab was behind my head. To my right was a long shelf, empty except for my vidscreen and a bottle of SmartWater.

Nearer the back, along the wall, was a metal square with a hinge on its bottom. To my left were two cabinets with metal latches. Between them was wall space filled with medical stuff—three-pronged electrical plugs, oxygen outlets, a blood pressure cuff, a biohazard box.

Now that I was fully awake, it was all very obvious. I had gotten sick. Kidnappers had taken me away in an ambulance, and they were keeping me in it, with the engine running.

For that to happen, the many layers of security around me had to have been breached; I had to have been betrayed by someone. But who?

Suddenly I heard a metallic latch snap, and the door at my feet opened. The sun flashed in, hurting my eyes. I squinted at the door and saw a black figure outlined there. He reached his hands inside the doorway and wriggled his long fingers to get a grip. He raised his knee up and stepped on the bumper. Then, with a lurch, he was inside and looming over me. Someone outside pushed the door shut again and latched it.

As soon as my eyes adjusted, I could see him clearly. He was a teenage boy, nearly two meters tall. His close-cropped hair nearly touched the metal ceiling. Did I know him? Had I seen his face before? I couldn't remember. With someone else inside, the ambulance seemed to shrink in size, and I felt the panic rising again. But the boy seemed to have no evil intentions. In fact, he gave no indication of seeing me at all. He reached toward the right wall and grabbed the top of the metal square. He pulled it forward, and it folded out into a bench seat with a leather bottom.

Once he sat down, I could only see his left side clearly. He snapped open a two-way vidphone and stared at it glumly, *stoically* (another Mrs. Veck word), like someone who was planning on sitting there for a long time.

Trying to remain calm, I concentrated hard on the boy. This is what I could tell: He was sixteen or seventeen. He was very thin, with gangly arms. His skin was very dark, like African dark. My father is a dermatologist, so I know skin. I know that his skin was that dark because his top four layers of derma had very active melanin molecules. His remaining three layers of derma were exactly the same as mine, as were all the other organs in his body.

I hoped he knew things like that. I hoped he had empathy for other people, like me. If he did, maybe I could talk to him, relate to him, one human being to another. He looked like he could go either way. He could either be a genuine human being or he could be one of those teenage African warlord soldiers who murder and rob and rape.

Right. Not a good thought, Charity. Teenage soldier rapists. Not the kind of thing you were trained to think about, is it? Get out of that mental place right away. Do something else. Try something. Anything. Try talking to him.

I glanced at my vidscreen clock—11:45. I tilted my head and shoulders up slightly, like I was doing crunches. I said, with as little fear as possible in my voice, "Is everything going all right? I mean, going as planned?"

He did not look up.

I continued, "I mean, is there anything I can do to help with the plan? Because that's what they teach us to do, to cooperate fully. My father feels that way, too. And Victoria and Albert feel that way. Because it's only currency, you know? Currency can be replaced. I cannot."

9

There was no answer. There was no reaction at all.

I waited a full minute; then I tried a different tack. "Excuse me. I have to go to the bathroom."

This was true, and it had an immediate effect. The boy folded up his two-way and stood, causing the hinged chair to snap back into the wall. He took two steps across the ambulance, reached into a cabinet, and pulled out a plastic bedpan with a roll of toilet paper inside it. He placed it on the stretcher, still without looking at me. He reached beneath the stretcher and snapped a metal latch, undoing the thick leather belt across my midsection. Then he opened the back door.

I gasped, "Wait a minute! What am I supposed to do with this?"

The boy stepped through the door and closed it behind him. Simultaneously, the red light of the vidcamera blinked off. Who was controlling it? I stared at it hard, waiting for it to come back on, but it did not.

I agonized for two minutes about what to do next. The truth was, I couldn't last much longer. I had no choice. I pushed through the humiliation of pulling down my pajama pants and sliding the bedpan under me. All the while, I kept one eye on the vidcamera. If it had come back on, I think I would have died right then. When I finished, I pulled the bedpan back out. With a wave of revulsion, I slid it as far away from me as I could on the stretcher.

A minute later, the door opened. But it wasn't the boy who stepped back in; it was Dr. M. Reyes.

I froze in place, terrified at the sight of him. He was dressed in green hospital scrubs, including a cap, a surgical mask, and tinted goggles. Clearly, there was no way I could ever identify him, except for the hint of oily black hair under his cap and the apelike way he moved. He never looked at me, as far as I could tell. He just picked up the bedpan and left.

As soon as he was gone, the boy returned. He pulled out his seat and resumed staring at the two-way screen. This was part of his job, obviously; part of the kidnapping plan. He was to keep watch on me and on whatever other scenes he had on that small screen.

Obviously, they were not worried that I would try to bolt. The boy didn't even bother to reattach the leather belt. Why should they worry? They had me surrounded.

I stared at him for a while longer, still seething from the humiliation of using the bedpan, still shaking from the close encounter with the menacing Dr. Reyes. I took a few minutes to just breathe and try to calm myself. What could I do? What should I do?

I couldn't just sit here and wait for Dr. Reyes to walk in and cut something out of my body. I had to act. I had to do *something* rather than nothing or I'd lose my mind. I reached over and clicked back into my "Kidnapping Industry" paper. The boy did not object; he did not stir at all. I scrolled until I found the section titled "Psychological Damage." This is what it said: "Many victims of kidnappings, although released without any obvious physical damage, may still suffer serious psychological damage." I thought about Hopewell Patterson. He was damaged goods, all right. "Damage occurs when a victim passes beyond normal fear into escalating states of panic, to hysteria, and then on to total psychological breakdown."

I clicked out of the document and concentrated as hard as

I could. I thought back to my anti-kidnapping classes. Most were taught by Highlands guards, but some were taught by Mrs. Veck. And one was taught by a psychologist, a pretty young woman in a blue suit. I pictured that woman in the classroom that day, and I tried to remember her words.

She said, "Use your mind to shut out fear."

She said, "Go to a safe place in your mind, to a memory of some kind. Pick a recent memory, so that it is still fresh."

She said, "Try to relive every minute of that memory—everything that happened; everything that you said and did. This will take you away, mentally, from your present fearful circumstances."

That was what she advised, so that's what I would do. I would *not* break down in this white metal prison. I would go someplace else in my mind. Someplace safe.

I concentrated hard. I thought back to a recent memory.

Friday, December 21. That was the last day of satschool. It was the day before the Christmas holidays began.

I would tell myself the story of that day, filling in every little detail. I would relive every part of my old life. By doing that, I would help myself get back to that life.

"An Edwardian
Christmas Celebration"

I remembered that December 21 was a cold day at my housing development, The Highlands, an estate community in Martin County, Florida.

I remembered that I began the day by helping Victoria with her morning chores. That was something I liked to do whenever no one else was around. My parents—that is, my father and my ex-stepmother—had recently divorced, but they still both lived in the house. It was a tense situation. I didn't blame them for spending most of their time away, and that worked just fine for me. I preferred to be with Victoria and Albert.

The first thing Victoria asked me every day was, "Did you sleep well, Miss Charity?"

This was not a casual question, and she already knew the

answer to it. I'd suffered for years from night terrors. To the kids at my school, to my parents, to practically everybody, I probably seemed a confident kid. But I was a sniveling coward at nighttime. I lived in fear of going to bed. I had horrible dreams that I thought were real. I woke up every night convinced that I was trapped in a cave, and that some monster was in there with me.

Only Victoria knew about this.

She had walked past my room one night and seen me sitting up in terror, drenched with sweat and gasping for air. She sat with me, saying little prayers and talking in a soothing voice until I fell back asleep. When I woke up later, she was still sitting there. And after that night, for three years, whenever I opened my eyes, she had been sitting there. I didn't know when she slept herself. But she was always in the kitchen, smiling and happy, when I came down for breakfast.

That's why I loved her so much. And that's why I tried to start each day by helping her do the dishes, even though it was against RDS regulations.

Anyway, Albert had disappeared after breakfast, and he had not returned. Just as Victoria and I had finished cleaning, we heard a loud buzzing sound, like a swarm of giant bumblebees. She rolled her eyes and smiled. "That's got to be Albert. Right?" She dried her hands and ducked into my bedroom, returning with a leather coat for me. "Here, Miss. You might catch cold outside."

Victoria then grabbed a gray cape and pulled it on over her black skirt and white blouse (her maid's outfit). I zipped my jacket up over my plaid Amsterdam Academy school jumper (my student's outfit). Then we hurried through the marble foyer and pushed open the red oak, stained-glass door.

Our front lawn was large even by Highlands standards, about twenty square meters. It was enclosed by a wrought-iron fence that ran from the helipad in our backyard to the cobblestone street in front.

Albert, dressed in his black suit, white shirt, and black tie (his butler's outfit), was crouched down on the left side of the flagstone walkway. He was tinkering with one of my father's toys, a Granville 440C drone helicopter. It was plastered, like all my father's toys, with University of Miami Hurricanes logos.

The 440C flew by remote control. It was similar to my father's real helicopter, including the Miami logos, except that it was one-fourth the size and it had no seats. It did have some neat capabilities, though, including a one-million-candlepower searchlight, a mounted vidcam with night vision, and a rescue bucket that could be lowered to pick up a package or, as the brochure pointed out, "to rescue a drowning kitten."

Albert turned and acknowledged us, muttering, "Miss Charity."

Albert was a big man—broad-shouldered, with a military bearing and a military-style shaved head. His first four layers of derma were light-colored, although there was a hint of African ancestry in the features of his face and in his general muscularness. Genetically, he was somewhat of a puzzle to me. He worked as our English butler, but he was probably of Caribbean origin.

Victoria, on the other hand, was clearly of Mexican origin. I didn't have to speculate about that. She once revealed to me, although it was against regulations, that she grew up in Mexico City. She was small and thin, but not at all frail. Her derma had a rosy brown tint, while her hair and eyes were lusciously dark. Patience and I agreed she was the most beautiful woman we had ever seen in person. She was Mexican, with an English name, but she worked as our French maid.

Victoria and Albert were both employed by the Royal Domestic Service, RDS—the largest and most prestigious company in the service industry. (I wrote a satschool paper about RDS, too.)

In the RDS hierarchy, Victoria was classified as a "one hundred percent employee." This meant that she lived with us around the clock, seven days a week, fifty-two weeks a year, except for the occasional emergency. One hundred percent employees got paid at the highest rate. Albert was classified as a "full-time employee." This meant that he was entitled to take days off, up to five per month. Albert usually took all five days. Depending on which of Patience's rumors you chose to believe, he spent that time either taking care of a house he owned somewhere or competing in professional chess tournaments.

Albert was working on attaching a metal box to the underside of the Granville 440C. He pointed at it and told me, "Ms. Meyers wants it to snow at your celebration today."

I commented, "Too bad we're in Florida."

He held up a securephone. "I just checked the weather alert; there's a chance of a thunderstorm later."

"That I'll believe." Then I asked him, "What's in the box? Fake snowflakes?"

He rapped his knuckles against the metal box, which had

a hinged top. "That's right. They're soap flakes. But when scattered by the drone's rotor blades, they'll flutter down just like snow."

Victoria smiled. "I would like to see that. I have never seen snow."

I told her, "Then you should come over to the Square."

"Me? No. I have no business being there today."

"You could say I forgot my lunch and that you were bringing it to me."

"Oh no. That would not be true."

"Okay. How about if I really forget it?"

"Miss Charity! I am not going to let you forget your lunch."

She was far too honest. I gave up. "Okay."

Just then, Albert pressed a button on a black control module. The rotors of the drone slowly came to life. He told us, "Step back, please. I have to log some flying time for the drone."

Victoria and I stood together on the flagstones and watched as the Granville revved up and then, with the push of another button, rose three meters into the air.

Albert stood with us, holding the controller in one hand and a thin metal vidscreen in the other. He held out the vidscreen to Victoria. "Here. You can watch on this. You can see what the Square looks like."

Victoria took the screen and turned it for both of us to see. Albert pushed another button and, suddenly, we were looking at the tops of our own heads on-screen, captured by the vidcam affixed to the drone.

The little helicopter rose higher and the vidscreen picture rose with it, showing all of our one-thousand-square-meter estate home with its red Spanish tiles, its ozone-screened pool and patio, its helipad, and the airstrip just beyond us to the south.

The drone shot up to a height of thirty meters and turned at a right angle. Then it darted off eastward, down our street, cruising over other estate homes—some with red tile roofs, some with green—until it reached the turrets of the guardhouse and banked left. In the distance, we could see the northern boundary of The Highlands, the St. Lucie Canal. The drone banked again, cruising over a row of homes with yacht moorings behind them, until it finally arrived at the Square.

The Square, which is officially called The Highlands Community Square, is part of a commercial area that occupies the entire west side of the development.

Victoria smiled happily at the sight of a dozen fake Christmas trees arranged in a circle around one very large real tree, a Scotch pine that had been trucked in right after Thanksgiving.

Albert let the drone hover there for a moment while Victoria took it all in. He told us, "This is where I'll press the eject button and the soap flakes will start flying out."

Victoria oohed like it had really happened.

I was more reserved.

Much more.

I dreaded the thought of another Mickie Meyers special being shot with me and my "friends," as Mickie called them. The fact was, I had only one friend at school, and that was Patience. Mickie kept showing up in our classroom, though, with her crew, and shooting us doing a bizarre array of activities. We hated it. (But her audience must have liked it. Her ratings were and are always high.)

We had just recovered from a bogus "Pilgrims' Thanksgiving Feast" with all-authentic foods during which the Dugan sisters, who are bulimic, actually took a break to vomit. The video feast ended with a heartwarming speech by Mickie about people from different backgrounds coexisting in peace and harmony. The actual feast ended with Patience Patterson overhearing a snide remark by Sierra Vasquez, becoming enraged, and pushing Sierra's face into a cranberry pie. Patience would not tell me what Sierra had said, but it must have been pretty bad.

Albert finally guided the drone homeward, back to the front yard, and landed it.

I called over to him, "Do you know when my ex-stepmother is getting here?"

Albert killed the drone's motor with a final button push. "Any time now, Miss Charity."

Victoria handed him back the vidscreen. She started walking toward the house, calling, "I'll get your backpack, Miss. It's almost time to go."

Albert locked the rotor blades of the drone by hand. Then he clicked open both doors of the garage, revealing my father's massive Mercedes 700D and our Yamaha 220 golf cart.

Although you were allowed to drive cars in The Highlands, most people used electric carts like our Yamaha to get around. Albert drove me to school in it every day. For a while, I insisted on walking the relatively short distance to the Square, but that meant that Albert had to walk with me with his Glock semi-automatic machine gun strapped behind his suit coat. Then he had to walk home. It was too much to ask. When we drove in the golf cart, he could at least store the Glock in the center console.

Well-trained, muscular butlers with semi-automatic weapons were the last line of defense against thieves, kidnappers, and other evildoers at The Highlands. The earlier lines of defense included the guards on patrol, the electric fences, the security cameras, and, of course, the GTDs.

The Highlands was considered, to be one of the securest developments in the United States. There was a waiting list of people willing to pay millions in currency to be among the 120 families who lived there.

Patience's father, Roy Patterson, was the top-selling realtor in Martin County. I had heard him offer my parents "cash on the barrelhead right here and right now," as he put it, for our estate house, but Mickie kept saying no. She is currently vidding a series called *Living with Divorce*. Once she has wrapped that project up, I expect her to move on. But you never know. She is relentless. And for the time being, I remain trapped in her world, a reluctant performer in her latest video reality series.

A sudden movement near my feet pulled me out of my thoughts and back to the ambulance. The dark boy was fidgeting around.

I watched him for a moment and realized that he had to go to the bathroom. After the bedpan incident, I had been extremely reluctant to drink anything. The dark boy had placed a bottle of SmartWater on the shelf next to my vidscreen, but I had not touched it. For all I knew, it was filled with drugs, or even poison.

The dark boy had a similar bottle on the floor next to him, which he sipped from regularly while staring at that screen. Those sips must have caught up with him, because he closed the two-way, stood up, and threw open the ambulance door. He looked out to the left and right. I figured he was trying to find someone to take his place. He turned toward me and made a face somewhere between the menacing snarl of a kidnapper and the pained expression of someone with a bursting bladder. Then he hopped out and slammed the door behind him.

My first thought was to try to escape. Could I throw open the door and make a run for it? My second thought, though, was about my training. The words came back to me verbatim: "An escape attempt is counterproductive. It may enrage the kidnappers. It may disrupt the ransom process, which is likely to be proceeding smoothly."

So I cleared my mind of escape thoughts. Instead, I reached over and activated my vidscreen. All output and input remained disabled. I scanned the titles of my files and spotted one that reminded me of Victoria and Albert. I needed to think about them for a while, so I clicked on it. Here is what it said:

The Royal Domestic Service, by Charity Meyers
Mrs. Veck, Grades 7–8
May 29, 2035

At the beginning of the twentieth century, the second most common career in the United States (after farmer) was domestic servant. Then this career disappeared almost completely due to new job opportunities and new household appliances introduced after World War II.

In the middle of the twenty-first century, however, the cycle has come around again, and *domestic servant* is once more a common career choice. Estate homes in particular require the presence of live-in help. To quote Mr. Roy Patterson of Patterson Realty, "Selling an estate home without servants' quarters is like trying to sell one without a currency vault. You just can't do it." The largest and most successful domestic servant company in the United States is Royal Domestic Service, or RDS.

My paper then included a link to a Royal Domestic Service brochure, which read: "RDS provides full-time, live-in servants for a variety of lifestyles." The brochure showed pictures of young, smiling RDS employees and descriptions of three types of plans (the comments in parentheses are mine).

For large families, the *Great-House Plan* provides four full-time servants:

- A butler (named something serious, like Edward or William)
- A maid (named something attractive, like Emily or Jasmine)
- A cook (named something French, like Henri or Louis)
- A chauffeur (named something practical, like James or John)

For small families, the *Estate Plan* provides two full-time servants:

- A maid/cook (ours is named Victoria)
- A butler/chauffeur (ours is named Albert)

For individuals, the *Townhouse Plan* provides one full-time servant:

- A maid/cook (see above for name choices)

For the *Estate Plan* (my family's plan), the brochure went on to explain:

> An RDS maid is not a cleaning woman, and an RDS butler is not a gardener. The maid cooks meals and attends to the children and to the lady of the house. The butler serves meals and attends to cars and to the gentleman of the house. The maid hires and supervises all other services for the interior, and the butler hires and supervises all other services for the exterior. In addition, RDS servants are rigorously trained to serve as paramedics and as bodyguards, and to serve a truly authentic English tea.

What they didn't put in the brochure, but what everyone knew, was that RDS servants were expected to protect the lives of their employers at all costs. That included, if necessary, dying in the line of duty.

Dying in the line of duty. That was another unhelpful, uncalming thought, and I kicked myself for having it. No dying. No. And no teenage soldier rapists. Get out of my mind!

I heard footsteps outside, so I turned from the vidscreen to watch the door. The dark boy entered, presumably relieved. He sure didn't look any happier, though. After a quick, cold glance at me, he resumed his silent screen-watching. I observed him for a minute. I even considered speaking to him, but his face was so hard-set that I decided against it.

Instead, I went back to my safety zone: to the minute details of my real life. I concentrated once more on the events of December 21.

I remembered that Mickie Meyers's airplane (which she piloted herself) landed at The Highlands' airstrip while Albert was driving me to satschool. You didn't have to be Sherlock Holmes to deduce when my stepmother was arriving. Her plane, a twenty-seat Gulfstream 50, had (and still has) MICKIE MEYERS painted on the side.

She and her crew always "hit the ground running," as she put it. They'd have their equipment set up shortly after Albert and I had rolled up to the row of townhouse office buildings on the Square. Albert dropped me off and watched attentively, Glock in hand, as I walked into the building that housed my satschool.

In theory, I attended the prestigious Amsterdam Academy, located on the Upper East Side of Manhattan. In actual fact, I went to school in a room with a mahogany conference table, eight executive chairs on rollers, and a large vidscreen connected by satellite to the real school in New York. And I was not alone in doing this. Other kids, clumped around other tables in other parts of the U.S., also attended this same satschool.

Our teacher, Mrs. Veck, had retired from the Chicago school system in order to move with her husband to The Highlands. She taught a combined seventh-and-eighth-grade class. In addition to her, we had a series of vidteachers in New York. Throughout the day, the scene on the vidscreen changed, from classroom to classroom and from teacher to teacher, but we never moved from our adjustable, ergonomic leather-match chairs.

As a result, I felt no more connected to the Amsterdam Academy than I would have to a school in a movie. Basically, I sat there with Patience and we gossiped all day about the boys we saw on the life-size screen. We tried to ignore everybody in our real classroom as best we could. We only semi-listened to the teachers on the screen, although we usually listened attentively to Mrs. Veck.

Mrs. Veck had agreed to take part in Mickie Meyers's latest bogus holiday program, titled "An Edwardian Christmas Celebration." She stood at the front of the room next to the smartboard and waited for us all to arrive. She had already placed a pile of calligraphy pens, markers, scissors, and card stock in the middle of the table.

To begin class, she held up a colorful Christmas card and rotated it so that we could all see. "Good morning, everyone. I am holding up a Christmas card from the Edwardian era in England, approximately from 1901 to 1910. Those were the years of the reign of King Edward the Seventh, the eldest son of Queen Victoria. Notice the use of red and green on the cards."

She picked up a second one. "Notice the red berries and the green holly, the red presents and the green Christmas trees. Our task is to create our own Christmas cards honoring the traditions of the Edwardian era. Who can tell me what some of those might have been?"

A lengthy pause followed. Mrs. Veck placed herself in this awkward position over and over again, several times a day, like a dog with an electric fence collar that keeps zapping itself. No one ever volunteered to answer. Ever. Then Mrs. Veck would begin at her right with Maureen Dugan and work her way around the table, attempting to elicit some intelligent remark from someone.

Patience and I would have had no trouble answering the question, but we didn't want to give the evil Dugans any ammunition. Mrs. Veck finally gave up and said, "How about tannenbaums, cherubs, Yule logs, stars, mistletoe, snow, sleighs? You can use any of these images as you create your cards. I will pass out several cards now for you to use as models."

She left her position and walked around the table, handing a card to each of us. My card showed a little girl in a red dress. She was lugging a snow-covered Christmas tree over her shoulder.

"Let's all get to work! We'll want to show Ms. Meyers eight lovely Edwardian Christmas cards when she arrives." Mrs. Veck then stepped out of the room, leaving us to our work. We all knew she hadn't gone far. The entire back wall was a two-way mirror behind which Mrs. Veck, or any parent observers, could sit and watch us. So we bent our heads and got to work.

The evil Dugan sisters sat right across from me. They were new to The Highlands. Some people thought they were twins because they looked so much alike, but they were actually born twelve months apart, to the day. (I always thought that was creepy. So did Patience.) Anyway, Maureen was the older one. She had been kept back because she couldn't read very well. Pauline was the younger one. She couldn't read, either. She sat next to Maureen, directly across from Patience. Both Dugan girls had dark fake tans penetrating their top two layers of derma. They both had fake blond hair, fake white smiles, and fake red nails. Could fake boobs be far behind?

The girl next to Pauline was Sierra Vasquez. Although she never exerted herself in any way, Sierra always had dark circles beneath her eyes and drooping lids above them. Her hobbies included sneering and muttering mean things to the Dugans about Patience and me. She was bony, with joints that actually showed through her skin at the knees and elbows, like the ends of broomsticks. Her short black hair was so intensely sprayed in place that she looked like she was wearing a bicycle helmet.

Whitney Rice was at the end of that side of the table. Whitney had very dry brown hair that she brushed straight out and sprayed in place so that it looked like lacquered straw. She had extremely broad shoulders, but skinny legs. She also had shifty eyes and a tendency to wear gingham, giving her the overall appearance of an untrustworthy scarecrow.

Sterling Johnston was the first person on our side of the table, one of the two boys. He was being treated for attention deficit disorder, as Mrs. Veck explained to us all in one of her "teachable moments." He was taking a drug called methylphenidate, which supposedly kept him focused, but which had an unfortunate side effect. Ever since the onset of puberty, Sterling had been relegated to the back of all class photos because of his tendency to be in a perpetual state of sexual excitement. This was evident whenever he was called on to go to the smartboard to write something. Patience and I avoided him, but the girls across the table sometimes pretended to drop things in order to look at him.

Hopewell Patterson, Patience's brother, was next. He was a tall boy with a uniform layer of excess body fat extending from his neck down to his ankles, giving him a sausage-like appearance (just like his father). His terrible posture and his low self-esteem made him appear to be spineless. I was always surprised when I saw him stand up, or walk, or do other common vertebrate things. Like everyone else, even I had succumbed to the obvious temptation to refer to him as "Hopeless."

Hopewell had been taken three years ago, right before the Pattersons moved to The Highlands. The kidnappers had cut off his left ear, and he had never really recovered from the experience, physically or psychologically. That area of his head was always covered by a clump of thick brown hair. There was a rumor in The Highlands that Patience had also been taken and that they had cut off her little toe. I knew that was not true, because Patience was my best friend and we had gone together for pedicures. Patience, fortunately, had inherited her mother's genetic traits. She was shorter and thinner than her brother (and three years younger—he had been kept back twice, due to poor grades). Patience had naturally blond hair, which she wore in cute, curly ringlets. Unlike her brother, she had excellent posture and a very feisty spirit. She also possessed the other hortatory name in the class.

Mrs. Veck had begun school last year with one of her teachable moments, an improvised lesson on hortatory names. I guess she meant well, but she basically ruined our lives. Mrs. Veck announced cheerfully that "a hortatory name is a name that embodies a virtue, such as Patience, or Charity, or Faith. Such names were very popular among the first Europeans who settled here, the Pilgrims."

The lesson went on from there, but the evil Dugans weren't listening. They had heard enough. From that day on, they referred to Patience and me as "the hors." We minded it at first, but then we kind of embraced the title.

I lay on my ambulance stretcher and thought about how they all looked, and how colorful the table looked, and how thin my own hands looked as I labored silently among them. I was the smallest member of the group, due to the fact that my mother had been only 1.5 meters tall and my father was 1.7. I had mousy brown hair, from my father's side, that I wore shoulder length. I had bright blue eyes that I kept cast down on my work. I had skinny legs, a freckled nose, and a tight mouth that would not smile, owing to the presence of braces.

After a while, a commotion behind the classroom mirror caused us all to stop coloring and cutting. I knew what it had to be, and I whispered to Patience, "It's Mickie."

Patience raised the right side of her lip. "Gross."

"Yeah. She'll be in and out for the next ten days."

"Is she going to make us be on her vidshow?"

I shook my head fatalistically. "Is the sun going to set in the west?"

Mickie Meyers threw open the classroom door and strode in. She was followed by her producer, a fierce-looking woman named Lena; then by her burly cameraman, Kurt; and finally by Mrs. Veck.

Most people get excited when they see Mickie Meyers in person. Her red rectangular glasses, her big white teeth, the prominent mole to the left of her mouth, have become fixtures on vidscreens across the U.S. Honestly, I can't understand what people see in her.

My relationship with Mickie hadn't changed much since the divorce. Very little had changed since then. Mickie had kept our last name. She explained to me that it was "for brand identity." I think she liked the alliteration, too. Victoria and Albert started calling her "Ms. Meyers" instead of "Mrs. Meyers." My dad started bad-mouthing her openly. That was about it.

Mickie used the kids in our class shamelessly for her education segments and her holiday segments and her family segments, and this day would be no exception. She shouted, "Hello, children! How is everybody?" Mickie didn't wait for a reply, but continued, "And a happy Christmas! A happy Edwardian Christmas. Right, Mrs. Veck?"

Mrs. Veck responded promptly, "That's right. The children have been working on cards—"

"So they have! Lovely. Charity, honey, let me see yours."

I held up my red-berry-and-green-holly creation for her to admire.

"Lovely. A lovely work in progress. And I see the rest of you are still hard at work on your works in progress, too. So here's what I'd like to do. Lena has a box of finished cards that she'll spread out on the table here. Go ahead, Lena. And Kurt will get some shots of all of you with your finished cards and your works in progress."

Lena and the cameraman quickly followed those instructions as my ex-stepmother continued, "Now, while you are finishing up, I'd like to record a comment or two about how an

Edwardian Christmas is different from a modern Christmas. Mrs. Veck, maybe you could lead a discussion of that."

Mrs. Veck smiled bravely. "Certainly. We were just discussing how the Edwardian era got its name. Who remembers that?"

After three seconds of dead airtime, Mickie filled in. "It was from King Edward. Right, Patience?"

Patience gulped. "Right."

"And which King Edward was it, honey? Was he the seventh?"

"Yes."

"Now why don't you put that all together for me into an answer for Mrs. Veck."

"It was King Edward the Seventh."

Mrs. Veck nodded gratefully as Kurt the cameraman squeezed around her and continued to shoot. "Now, who can tell us how these cards differ from our modern cards?"

During the silence that followed, Mickie Meyers directed the cameraman to vid certain specific cards. Then she looked right at me and raised her penciled eyebrows high, indicating that I should provide the answer.

At that moment, Sierra mumbled something to Pauline.

Patience seized the opportunity to suggest, "I think Sierra knows."

"Really? Okay, Sierra. You go ahead, honey."

Sierra pulled her lips back in an enormous sneer, like a cornered raccoon. "I didn't say anything."

"You didn't? Well, how about saying a line for the segment, like 'Have a happy Edwardian Christmas'?"

"I'm not gonna say that."

"No? What would you like to say?"

"Nothing."

"How about you, Pauline?"

"Nothing. This is stupid."

"Oh! Come on, girls. I saw you working hard on the cards. Hopewell? Do you want to say something in the segment?"

Hopewell let his head slide down to the right, and it remained in that position until Mickie gave up. "Okay, Charity. It looks like it's back to you."

I mumbled "As usual" as Kurt lined up his shot. Patience, ever faithful, slid closer and looked into the camera with me as we intoned, "Have a happy Edwardian Christmas."

Mickie appeared to be satisfied with our greeting, insincere as it was. She immediately dispatched Kurt to the Square to set up for the second half of the shoot. She added, "Mrs. Veck, you and the children should follow quickly. All right? Each child should bring a finished card, one of the nice ones that Lena gave them. And a clothespin. Lena, do you have those?"

Lena reached into a coat pocket and produced a handful of red and green clothespins, which she tossed onto the table. Then she and Mickie hurried out.

I got jolted back to the present by a sound directly behind me, the sound of the ambulance cab door opening. This was followed by a violent sound, like someone's head had been pushed into the cab wall.

I ventured a quick look past my feet. The dark boy was no longer there!

I heard a gruff, accusing voice from inside the cab. "You were asleep!"

Then I heard a weary voice. "No."

"Shut up! Don't lie to me, or . . ."

My whole body tensed. I pictured the evil face of Dr. Reyes.

The weary voice protested, "I was right here. She could not get past me."

"You were asleep!"

"Just for one second."

"You are to be awake every second!"

"It is way past my shift. It is Monnonk's shift now."

"I will tell you when your shift is over. Understand?"

"Yes."

"Do you know what I will do if I catch you again?"

The voice didn't answer.

Dr. Reyes continued, "You will never see it coming. One needle and it will be over. Do you understand now?"

The voice whispered hoarsely, "Yes, sir. Yes, Doctor."

The door then slammed shut. Whoever was sitting in the front stayed completely quiet for five minutes. And so did I.

At last I let myself relax. I lay back and stared at the ceiling. My heart was racing; my mind was racing. I had to do something right away or I might have a full-blown panic attack, like a wide-awake night terror.

I rolled my head left and right, staring at the surrounding white walls of the ambulance. I pressed my hands against my temples, forcing myself to think about the white walls back at the satschool. What exactly did they look like? What was hanging on them? I remembered. Mrs. Veck's posters were hanging on them—inspirational sayings beneath cute animal photos. A kitten clinging to a branch with the caption "Hang in there." A

grumpy bear looking out from a cave: "We all have bad days."
An eagle gliding in a bright blue sky: "Let your dreams soar."

I saw them all in my mind. And I was back in that class-room again, on that Friday morning.

Mrs. Veck instructed us to gather our materials and to follow her out into the Square. She added, rather desperately, "Let's all do our best to help Mrs. Meyers with her program." That was an uncharacteristic slip of the tongue for Mrs. Veck, but it bothered me. I always resented hearing Mickie referred to as "Mrs. Meyers."

My mother, the real Mrs. Meyers, died when I was seven. She died during my first week in second grade. Back then, we lived in Lake Worth, Florida, about forty kilometers south-east of The Highlands. We lived in a regular housing develop-ment, not in an armed military compound, and I attended a real school, not a satschool.

But my mother, who was a nurse, died of skin cancer, a melanoma lurking beneath her hairline that she never no-ticed. Neither did her husband, my father, a trained dermatol-ogist. It all happened very quickly. From the first sign that something was wrong to her death was exactly 103 days. I counted them out on a calendar.

I remember my father being totally devastated by her illness. I wasn't devastated at first. I was just confused, and then numb.

I remember my mother near the end actually urging my father, in front of me, to remarry. She told him, "Charity will need a mother. As soon as possible."

But my father, as it turned out, had another plan. He

spent the three years following my mother's death working at home, nearly around the clock. He threw himself body and soul into dermatological research. He became a hermit hiding in his room, scanning hundreds of content files for papers published in the field.

Then, when I was in fifth grade, he emerged from his research cave to introduce a skin treatment called DermaBronze. When applied to the top two layers of derma by a trained physician during a ten-minute procedure, DermaBronze provided "a deep, medically safe tan for up to fifteen months."

The DermaBronze treatment made us rich, and it made my father briefly famous. He was deluged with offers to appear on vidcontent shows, and he grudgingly started accepting those offers.

That's where my future ex-stepmother came into the picture.

Mickie Denman (her name at the time) graduated from the University of Florida with an M.S. in psychology. She opened her own office in Hobe Sound and counseled rich women about their mental health problems. She wrote an advice column for rich women based on her (slim) experience, but it was a big hit. The column got picked up by a content provider, and her name started to appear on vidscreens around central and south Florida.

Soon her face started to appear, too, as she became an occasional guest for a medical show called *Living with* . . . Then she got her big break. She was asked to fill in for three days as the host of that show. The third of her three episodes was about the amazing new technique called DermaBronze. My father appeared with her that day, and the rest is history.

My father never knew what hit him. Mickie says that she dazzled him with her charms. I guess that's possible. I say he had just been working too hard for too long in his lonely room.

Anyway, within a week they started slipping away together to the islands, leaving me with a series of professional sitters. Within ninety days (I counted that out on a calendar, too), they had gotten married, and my new stepmother was hosting nationwide content shows as "Mickie Meyers."

Shortly after that, we moved to The Highlands. As they explained it to me, we had no choice but to move to a newer house in a better neighborhood. Our old house had been built before the World Credit Crash, so all we had to safeguard our currency was a steel safe bolted to the floor. We now needed a modern currency vault built into an inside wall, and many layers of electronic surveillance, and a private security patrol, all because my dad was rich and my stepmother was famous.

But I hated The Highlands. I had no friends there. All I did was hide in my room. In my solitude, I finally started to grieve for my mother and to miss her terribly. That's when Victoria arrived in my life. Victoria was there to help me during that period; my father and Mickie were not. They could have been, but they were not.

Since those days, Mickie has gone global as the new host of the *Living with* . . . series of broadcasts. The first one was based on me and my departed mother: *Living with Loss.* The second was *Living with Stepchildren.* I guess that was partly about me, too, but I wasn't in it. Her third, *Living with Divorce,* is still unfolding. I play at least a small role in that one.

Mickie's parent corporation, SatPub, has its headquarters in New York City, so she spends most of her time there. On Friday, December 21, however, she was in The Highlands, in the Square, directing her crew's actions on the ground and directing Albert's drone helicopter in the air.

Whoever had decorated the public places in The Highlands was taking orders directly from Mickie. The theme in the Square was "An Edwardian Christmas." There were twelve two-meter trees arranged around the nine-meter Scotch pine. Each of the twelve trees was decorated with items from one of the Twelve Days of Christmas—partridges, pear trees, et cetera. In addition, in front of the Sun Currency Bank was a golf cart that had been converted to a sleigh, complete with reindeer and a Santa (although I don't think there was anything particularly Edwardian about that).

Everything was in its place and ready to go when my class arrived. Mrs. Veck tried to form us into a line, but Pauline Dugan made a fuss about standing in front of Sterling Johnston, shouting, "I'm not standing by any pervert!" and causing Kurt to momentarily turn off his camera. Mickie then took over, arranging us in a semicircle and cautioning Kurt to shoot Sterling's top half only.

On Mickie's signal, the Coventry Carol blared out of a speaker, the snowflakes started to flutter down, and one by one, we walked up to the Scotch pine and attached our Christmas cards with the colored clothespins. As this was going on, Mickie recorded a preliminary voice-over. She then walked in front of the big tree and recorded an intro and an outro. It was all over by 10:00 hours, which was lucky for Mickie because that's when my father's helicopter arrived.

I spotted it first, descending toward our helipad at the southwest corner of the development. It was easily recognizable by the orange-and-green Miami Hurricanes logos. Everything would have been fine if it had just kept going down for a landing. Unfortunately, though, my father must have spotted his 440 drone hovering above the Square and decided to investigate. The helicopter, a Robinson Beta Five, rose up again and tilted in our direction.

Mickie spotted the helicopter and called over to Albert, "What's going on? What's he doing here?"

Albert directed the drone away from us to a new spot above the security wall. He shook his head. "I don't know, Ms. Meyers."

"You didn't expect him?"

"I didn't. He hasn't called me. He hasn't even filed a flight plan for today."

Mickie clenched her fists. "Terrific."

Then Mickie, the crew, we students, and a few onlookers stood and watched as the big helicopter roared up over the Square and held its position. I could see my father's face twenty meters above us. He had a goofy expression on, like he might have started drinking early, or like the previous night's party hadn't yet ended. He gave a thumbs-up sign to the crowd below and hovered there in the blue sky like Mrs. Veck's inspirational eagle.

That's when it happened.

The Edwardian Christmas cards, caught up in the wind from the rotors, began to snap off the big tree and swirl around the Square like so many colored and calligraphed pieces of litter. Then other items from other trees fell victim to the wind and let go—small plastic pears, partridges, French hens, turtledoves. They all ripped away from their hooks and got caught up in the vortex of swirling soap flakes, dirt, and paper. The Santa sleigh and reindeer fell over next. Finally, the twelve trees in the circle succumbed, bending like palms in a hurricane until they snapped off their bases and started flopping about crazily on the ground.

After a few more chaotic seconds, the helicopter roared away and returned to the helipad, leaving all that devastation in its wake. Only the Scotch pine remained in place, but it had been stripped of all its balls and stars and other ornaments. Hundreds of meters of Christmas tree lights now hung from the branches in twisted clumps, frayed and broken, spitting orange sparks of fire on the ground and into the air.

Mickie could no longer contain herself. She screamed, "That idiot!" She turned to Albert and ranted, "What is he doing here? Why isn't he on some golf course? Or at some football game?"

Albert guided the drone downward to safety, landing it on a clear patch of pavement in front of the bank. He answered calmly, "I don't know, Ms. Meyers."

Mickie redirected the rant to her producer and her cameraman, making very unflattering comments about my father as they loaded their gear on a cart. Then they all drove quickly back toward the airstrip.

I looked around at the demolished Square. Everywhere was chaos, a condition rarely seen and never tolerated at The Highlands.

Taking advantage of the momentary breakdown in law and order and the lack of adult supervision, Maureen and

Pauline Dugan suddenly ran toward Hopewell and jumped onto his back, knocking him down. They turned him over and pinned him to the ground behind one of the small trees. Maureen sat on Hopewell's shoulders, immobilizing him, while Pauline reached over and pulled his clump of hair back, exposing his left ear.

Pauline shouted, "Oh, gross!" and pretended to gag.

Maureen made a horrible face, too, as Sierra and Whitney leaned in to see.

Patience yelled over to me, "Come on!" and we ran through the debris to help him.

I must admit I was shocked myself by the sight of Hopewell's ear. I had never seen it before. I had never even thought about asking to see it. As far as I was concerned, it was a secret that should stay a secret.

But there it was.

It looked like a rotten apple, or a shriveled rose. It was bright red, like a wound, and it curled up at the edges like its skin was dying. It was like no ear I had ever seen before. (Patience told me that when Hopewell was returned by the kidnappers, he had nothing more than an open sore on the side of his head. Her parents were desperate for something, anything, to replace what had been there. Mr. Patterson found a donor to provide an ear right away, no questions asked, for a lot of currency.)

Patience stood over both Dugans and screamed at the top of her lungs, "Get off of him!"

I echoed her. "Yeah! Get off! Let him go!"

Maureen Dugan didn't even look up. "Get lost, hors."

Patience, without hesitation, threw herself on top of

Pauline, so I did the same to Maureen. Neither of us could fight very well, but our momentum was strong enough to knock the Dugans back.

Hopewell rolled over and crawled away on his elbows.

Maureen Dugan grabbed my hair and snapped my head back so that I couldn't move. I could see that Pauline Dugan had Patience in a headlock, too. Then Mrs. Veck ran up, shouting, "Girls! Girls! Things are bad enough without this horseplay going on. You stop right now!" After a few seconds the Dugans, each with a final twist, let our heads go, and peace was restored.

The guard patrol arrived just then in a machine-gun-mounted van. Two men in black uniforms jumped out and surveyed the situation. One pointed to some downed electrical wires. The other one shouted, "Everybody out of the Square! Right now!"

Mrs. Veck led us on a quick march back into our classroom, where we all sat in stony silence. Patience and I stared defiantly at the Dugans; Sierra and Whitney sneered; Hopewell hung his head miserably; and Sterling Johnston seemed lost in thought.

Mrs. Veck turned on the vidscreen. She managed a tight smile. "Well, that was interesting. Now it's time for us all to join the Amsterdam Academy for the holiday celebration up in New York."

The screen showed eight scenes of kids sitting at eight mahogany tables, scattered all over the U.S., staring at vidscreens of their own.

They all looked miserable.

* * *

The dark boy was back. I heard him muttering into his two-way. I could pick up very few distinct words; the rest was an audio blur. I believed he was speaking Haitian Creole. That would have made sense. He had the derma and the physical features common to Haitians. I listened hard, trying to sense his mood, trying to pick a time to engage him in conversation.

Finally, he picked the time himself. He folded up the two-way, turned, and looked right at me. We held this stare for perhaps ten seconds. I expected him to speak at any moment, but he did not.

I finally took it on myself to start. I asked, "Do you speak English, too?"

His lip curled into a sneer. Was he angry? Was he going to hurt me? He wouldn't answer at first, but I steadfastly maintained eye contact, so he finally gave in. He replied, in clear, unaccented English, "Of course I do. What kind of question is that?"

"Well, I only heard you speaking, you know, Creole."

"I see. So you figured I just fell off the banana boat."

"No."

"You figured I just floated here on a piece of wood, with my nineteen brothers and sisters, my *frès* and *sès*—"

"No. Not at—"

"To find a better life in America, cleaning your toilet bowl after you just used it." His tone of voice was calm, but his words were angry, and they frightened me. I had definitely offended him. Deeply. Might he get up? Might he hit me, or worse? There was certainly no one around to stop him.

I quickly stammered, "I'm sorry. I heard you speaking one

language. I should not have assumed that you did not speak another one. You speak it very well, I might add."

His sneer returned. "Listen to you. You are still assuming."

"What?"

"Now you assume that I am incapable of speaking any language other than English, the language of the slave master. Isn't that right?"

I started to deny it, but I stopped myself. I had to win this boy's confidence somehow. I decided to tell him the truth. "Yes. You're right. I did assume that. And I apologize again."

The truth had a definite positive effect on him. The sneer dropped. He asked me, *"Parlez-vous français?"*

"Uh, no, actually. I don't speak French. I speak a little Spanish. I want to learn French. We can take it next year, in high school, and I do want to."

"C'est ma première langue."

"Uh, sorry, I didn't get that."

"It is my first language."

"Oh. I see. And Creole is your second?"

The sneer returned, but at half strength. "No. English is my second. Creole is something I picked up recently. And it's not a language, in my opinion. It's a creole."

My mind raced, trying to come up with a good reply. And failed. Instead, I heard myself repeating a line from Mrs. Veck: "You can't define a word using the same word."

His brown eyes looked right into mine. They were very intelligent eyes. I hadn't noticed that before. He said, "They are different words if you see them on paper. One has a capital *C,* and one has a small *c. Comprendez-vous?"*

"No," I admitted.

"The word *Creole,* with the capital *C,* describes Haitian Creole as a civilized language worthy of capitalization, just like French or English. But in fact it is not a civilized language. It is a creole, with a small *c,* which is defined as a civilized language mixed with the language of a savage tribe. In the case of Haitian Creole, you have the language of the civilized masters, the French, mixed with the languages of the many African tribes that they enslaved. No disrespect to my *frès* and *sès,* but their language is a textbook example of a creole with a small *c.*" He paused to let that sink in with me.

I said, "Well, thank you. I didn't know that."

He turned away, very satisfied with himself.

I had the impression he was about to resume ignoring me, so I decided to ask him something else. Anything else. "Uh, does that guy on the other end of the phone speak French, too?"

I waited quite a while for a reply, but he finally did say, "No. None of them speak French. They speak Creole and Spanish, mostly. And some English. Bad English."

"Yeah? Yeah, I'll bet. How about you, though? How come you speak English so well?"

I thought it was a harmless question, but his lip curled up again into a full sneer. "I see. Well, there is a simple explanation for that. I was plucked from the ocean by an eccentric white billionaire, who bet another eccentric white billionaire that he could teach me to speak better English than King William."

I couldn't tell if he was really angry or simply mocking me. I assumed he was angry. "I'm sorry again. I didn't mean to offend you—"

"I am not at all offended. It is a typical rich-white-girl re-action. You look at me and figure I cannot do anything requiring a brain."

"No. I don't think that. I—"

"For your information, I speak English because I am a citizen of the United States, a primarily English-speaking nation."

"Well, sure. Okay. So what about the French?"

He shook his head slowly. "Forget it. You don't need to know anything about that."

"But I want to."

"Why? So you can tell the FBI about it? So you can have me caught, tried, and executed by lethal injection? I don't think so." He didn't say anything else for a few seconds. Then he remembered something. "Oh yeah. I have a message from Dr. Reyes. He said you can sit up now, if you want. He said the sedative has passed through your system."

"Oh, I see. Thank you. Does Dr. Reyes talk to you in English?"

He didn't reply, but I thought I saw him smirk.

I pulled myself up into a sitting position. Then I reached around the stretcher and found a latch. I raised up the back piece of the stretcher and affixed it so that I was now seated at a ninety-degree angle. I felt so much better that I spoke to him again, conversationally, without even thinking about it. "Well, I want to be able to do what you do, to speak different languages. I want to learn French and Spanish. And Creole, too."

"Pourquoi?"

" 'Why'? Does that mean 'why'?"

"Oui."

"Because Creole is spoken here in Florida. I want to know the languages that are spoken around me."

He didn't reply.

"Would you teach me a few words in Creole?"

After a pause he said, "Sure. Why not? Here's all the Creole you'll ever need to know: *Vòlè* means 'thief.'"

I repeated it phonetically: "Vo-lay."

"*Mantlè* means 'liar.'"

"Mant-lay. Okay. Great. Now can you tell me some good-thing words?"

He snorted. "Good-thing words? Is that even English? Listen: the Haitians around here don't use little-white-girl, 'good-thing' words. For example, they have no word for 'heli-pad,' or 'yacht basin,' or 'satschool.' Those are words in common use in The Highlands, correct?"

"You're right," I admitted.

"Probably the only Creole you have ever heard came from the lawn guy, or the garbage man. Both of them were, I am sure, complaining about you, the masters, as they muttered along in their slave language."

"That's not right. We don't treat people like slaves."

"If they work in The Highlands, they work under the constant watch of guards with machine guns; they must step carefully around electric fences; their every move is recorded on vidcams as they do your dirty work."

"I do my own dirty work. I have my own set of chores, and then I help Victoria do hers when no one is around."

"Victoria. Is she your family's slave?"

"No!" This time, I was the one who didn't speak for a while. I finally managed to say, "Victoria is my favorite person in the world. She is like my mother. She is nobody's slave."

He rolled his eyes. I ignored that and continued. "She works for RDS, and she makes a lot of money. She is saving it so she can go to college someday and become an attorney."

When he replied, it was without sarcasm. "It sounds like you admire her."

"I do."

"And you trust her."

"Completely. With my life."

"Then why do you have a vidcam in her bedroom?"

I stopped to think. How did he know that? Then I protested, "That's got nothing to do with us. That's RDS policy. And she doesn't mind it."

"She doesn't?"

"No."

"Has she said that?"

"No. But I know she doesn't. I know her."

"You do?"

"Yes."

"All right. What's her real name?"

I froze. Flustered, I finally stammered, "I — I don't know."

"I see."

"She doesn't use her real name at work."

"I see. And why should she, when she has a perfectly good slave name?" I opened my mouth to protest, but he cut me off. "The entire situation is ridiculous. You don't know the first thing about her, which is her name. She pretends to be your little French maid, or English, or whatever. That's all you know. You know a fictional character." He turned back to the two-way with finality, signaling the end of our conversation.

That was fine with me. I didn't want to hear him bad-mouthing Victoria anymore.

I sat back and looked at my vidscreen. The blue numerals read 13:13, and the red light was on. I stared into it, trying to imagine who was watching. I figured that the kidnappers were sending a vid image to my father, to scare him. They were showing him the pathetic, sniveling victim, in her little-girl footed pajamas, waiting desperately for the currency to be delivered. It was all standard operating procedure for kidnappers.

I knew their game, all right.

I just hoped my father did.

Rituals of
Social Inversion

Haitian? Spanish? Was one of the kidnappers working inside The Highlands, pretending to be a lawn guy? Or a garbage man? I doubted it. All workers at The Highlands, according to the brochure, were "rigorously screened, using FBI databases."

So where would a kidnapper have the chance to see me outside of The Highlands? How had I been targeted? Then I remembered. And I felt foolish, because it was so obvious! The kidnapper had seen me in Mangrove on Kid-to-Kid Day, an event co-sponsored by The Highlands and the town of Mangrove.

Kid-to-Kid Day actually began with Patience Patterson and me. Patience overheard her maid, Daphne, taking an emergency phone call. (RDS employees are forbidden to talk about their outside lives to clients.) Daphne's family, who lived in Mangrove, had lost their house and all their belongings in a grease fire. Patience and I decided to help them, rules be damned.

We snooped around in Mr. Patterson's vidfiles and learned where Daphne really lived. Then we accessed the Martin County Fire and Rescue database. We learned that Daphne's younger siblings—twin girls in fifth grade, a boy in seventh grade, and a boy in ninth grade—had lost every stitch of clothing except what was on their backs when they ran from the house.

Patience and I, without Daphne's knowledge, pulled out lots of our own clothes and put them in two large bags. Then we visited families in The Highlands who had seventh- and ninth-grade boys. When we were through, we had four big bags of shirts, pants, sneakers, dresses, et cetera.

Our next step was to figure out how to deliver them. Daphne would not be allowed to accept anything from us. She wasn't even allowed to tell us that she had a family, or that she had a real name. So we asked Mr. and Mrs. Patterson what to do. At first they were mad at Daphne for taking a personal call in a place where Patience might overhear her. But then Mr. Patterson saw a business opportunity. He offered to take the four bags to Mangrove and to deliver them personally to the mayor if my stepmother, Mickie Meyers, would agree to vid the event for her show.

Mickie jumped at the chance. She arranged for Daphne's four siblings, their parents, and the mayor of Mangrove to be standing outside the burned-out shell of the house when Mr. Patterson arrived in his bulletproof car, followed by two Highlands security guards in their van.

Mr. Patterson presented the bags to the kids as Kurt's camera ran. Then, to Mr. Patterson's surprise, the kids gave him something in return. It was a *tornada*—a wooden doll with the letter *P* carved in the front and a face carved on the back. One of the twin girls explained to him that the doll symbolized her wish to see him again someday and to return the favor.

Mickie's vidcast of the event was such a success that both The Highlands and the town of Mangrove decided to do it again the following year. They didn't have another burned-out family, so Mickie came up with the idea of using kids from my class and kids from the town in an event she titled "Kid-to-Kid Day." That outing went smoothly, too, except for an incident where a town kid, some mean boy, tripped Hopewell and gave him a bloody nose. Albert cleaned Hopewell up quickly, though; the vidcast went on as planned; and it scored more high ratings.

As a result, the third annual Kid-to-Kid Day was scheduled for Saturday, December 22. It turned out to be a very full day—full of people, and events, and details. It was exactly the kind of day that I needed to focus on. I made up my mind to concentrate next on Saturday, December 22.

I remembered that the students from my class gathered in the Square at 09:00. The group included Sierra, the Dugans, Sterling Johnston, Hopewell, Patience, and me. (Whitney's family had already headed south in their yacht to spend the holidays in the Berry Islands.)

By 09:15, our group of seven kids, four maids, four butlers, two guards, one realtor (Mr. Patterson), and one teacher had loaded up sixteen bags of clothing into the storage bay of the security van. Lena also handed Mrs. Veck two cartons of books for young readers—all Ramiro Fortunato novels—from the book division of SatPub, Mickie Meyers's parent corporation.

The Highlands' van was a long gray scary-looking vehicle. It was more like a bus than a van, customized with armor, bombproof sides, and black-tinted, bulletproof windows. It seated between twenty and twenty-five people, depending on the configuration. For this trip, the guards had removed the top-mounted machine gun and stowed it on a rack to the right of the driver, eliminating two seats in the process.

The four butlers—Albert, William, Edward, and James—went over the security plans with the guards. Each butler would carry a Glock 450C, an NLS (non-lethal stun) gun, and an aerosol can of organic repellent. None of these weapons had been used the previous two years, but they decided to keep them in the security plan just in case.

This was to be the first Kid-to-Kid Day for the Dugans. They seemed to have no clue what the day, the field trip, or the gift exchange was all about. Pauline snarled at Mrs. Veck, "Why do we have to go? This sounds so stupid."

Mrs. Veck smiled kindly. "Well, Pauline, you girls did return your permission slips. They were signed by both of you and by your parents. That permission slip described the trip in great detail. Didn't you read it?"

"No."

"Why?"

"I don't know. It was too long."

I commented to Patience, "That, and the fact that she can't read."

Pauline snarled, "Shut up!"

Maureen stepped forward. "Maybe I'll snap your scrawny neck, hor."

Patience lined up next to me. "Maybe you won't, dumbass."

Mrs. Veck interrupted: "Girls, girls. This is a day for giving. And it's a day for learning."

This time it was Maureen who snarled, "Learning? It's Saturday. And we're supposed to be on Christmas break."

Mrs. Veck replied, "All school field trips are about learning. And this trip will provide some excellent opportunities. Do you remember our discussion yesterday about King Edward the Seventh?" All of us looked away. She continued, "Well, we'll be talking about him some more, and about his parents, and about Christmas traditions. A lot of our Christmas traditions come from Edward's family, and from his era."

At that moment, Mickie Meyers, Lena, and Kurt the cameraman pulled up in an electric cart. Mickie shouted at us, "Everybody ready to roll?" She didn't wait for a reply, which is good, because it would have been a long wait. She led her group onto the van, and the rest of us followed.

I sat with Patience near the middle. Mrs. Veck told the rest of the students to sit around us so that she could lecture on the way. Mickie and Kurt set up in the aisle to shoot her speeches and our reactions, should there be any.

Finally the maids and butlers climbed on and dispersed themselves throughout the van. Albert came down the aisle to check our ID cards. These cards, issued by the federal government, were embedded with microchips that contained our personal information. They also served as global tracking devices for any kids who didn't have them implanted. (Supposedly the cards were hard to come by, but the Dugans bragged that they had cards to prove they were eighteen years old and that they had used them to drink in Bermuda.)

When he'd finished his check, Albert gave a thumbs-up signal to the guard in the driver's seat and we took off. We drove parallel to the north wall of The Highlands, on the bank of the St. Lucie Canal. Families who lived along the north wall, like Whitney's, could sail directly from The Highlands to the Intracoastal Waterway. From there they could turn north toward Amelia Island, or south toward Fort Lauderdale, or they could continue east to the Atlantic Ocean and beyond. ("Beyond," however, included some areas controlled by pirates, so people tended to stick to a few safe destinations.) My house was on the south wall. It was not literally a wall, though. It was an airstrip surrounded by an electronic security fence.

This field trip was a rare outing for us. Highlands kids didn't often get to travel beyond the walls. School came to us via satellite links. Shopping was done online and then delivered to us by tightly screened UPS or FedEx trucks. Even doctors came to us in special security ambulances.

Once we got past the guardhouse gate, we accelerated toward the Florida Turnpike, and Mickie signaled Kurt to start shooting. She raised her microphone and began, "I'm Mickie Meyers. And we are privileged to ride along with Mrs. Veck's class on Kid-to-Kid Day, a wonderful tradition that began here three years ago. On Kid-to-Kid Day, children from The Highlands, a wealthy Martin County development, bring clothes to children living in Mangrove, an impoverished local town. In return, the children of Mangrove give the Highlands children handmade gifts."

Mickie took a step toward Mrs. Veck. "I am told that this type of day has its origins in the past, and that it may even tie in with our discussion yesterday about an Edwardian Christmas. Isn't that right, Mrs. Veck?"

"That's right."

"And just who was this King Edward who gives his name to our theme?"

"He was the son of Queen Victoria and her husband, Prince Albert. They are generally spoken of together, as a couple—Victoria and Albert."

Mrs. Veck paused briefly, reaching one hand out and waving it to get Sterling Johnston's attention. She then continued, "Prince Albert, a German, brought many Christmas traditions to England that are now thought to be English. Queen Victoria loved those traditions and practiced them over her long life."

Mickie wasn't really listening. She was watching the scene unfold on Lena's screen. But she made a rotating motion with her hand, urging Mrs. Veck to keep talking, so she did.

"Many of our modern customs come to us from that era. And some stem from a very interesting phenomenon that happened at Christmastime known as *the ritual of social inversion.* The king or lord always had food and drink left over from the fall harvest that was just sitting there, about to spoil. So, in the first days of winter, he shared it with the poor people, the peasants. The peasants, for a few days at least, got to live like lords."

Mrs. Veck turned to us. "Now, students, how might that phenomenon, the ritual of social inversion, relate to Christmas?"

Patience actually raised her hand and answered: "We give to the poor at Christmas, like on this trip to Mangrove."

"Yes indeed. That's a good modern example. But who can look back with me for many centuries—for 2,035 years?"

I had no idea where Mrs. Veck was going with this, so naturally she called on me: "Charity?"

I tried: "Uh, the birth of Jesus, maybe?"

"The birth of Jesus indeed! A poor baby. Now, who bowed down to Jesus on the first Christmas?"

"The Three Kings?"

"That's right. Three wealthy kings bowed down to one poor baby! Many Spanish cultures consider Three Kings' Day, El Día de los Reyes, to be an essential part of Christmastime, the day when the poor and the meek are honored in a ritual of social inversion. In fact, the town of Mangrove celebrates its Christmas Carnaval on that day."

Mickie interrupted. "What does this have to do with Victoria and Albert?"

"Well, Victoria and Albert enthusiastically embraced the ancient rituals of Christmastime, and they brought those rituals into modern London society. And from there the customs traveled to the New World, to our world."

Mickie nodded briefly. Then she signaled to Kurt to stop shooting and moved to a front seat, next to Lena.

Patience told me, "I did a paper on Victoria and Albert. They had it all. They were the richest, most powerful, most glamorous couple in the world. They were even happy! But Albert died forty years before Victoria. She spent all that time mourning him and building monuments to him, monuments of her love. That's what I want some guy to do for me."

"Marry you and then die?"

"Marry me. Love me desperately. And then die. Then I'll build monuments to our love."

We continued driving east past Indian Well, a former migrant town that housed workers for the many wealthy communities in the county. From the van window, I could see rusty trailers, small cinder-block homes, and RVs that would never ride again. We passed a lake called Deep Lake, preceded by signs that advertised its "great bass fishing."

Sierra told Maureen, "My dad says that Deep Lake is stocked with killer bass fish. They'll eat anything that falls in there."

Patience and I started to scoff at her, but Mrs. Veck surprised us by saying, "That's true, Sierra. In fact, they used to call it Killer Bass Lake. Who can tell me why they might have changed that name?"

After a moment, she gave up: "No one? How about to make it more appealing and more marketable to fishermen?"

Everyone avoided eye contact with her. "Okay, then. Let's all look across the lake. That means you, too, Sterling Johnston. Now, what do you think those huge metal towers are on the other side?"

I looked where she was pointing. The south side of the lake was bordered by a row of tall steel structures. I gave Mrs. Veck a break. "Those are high-tension electrical wires."

"Yes. Thank you, Charity. Who can tell me what their purpose is?"

Maureen actually made a comment: "Don't those have

electromagnets or something that come out of them and eat your brain? Don't kids down here have, like, a hundred times more brain tumors than we do?"

Mrs. Veck smiled. "I don't know, Maureen. Would you like to research that information and share it with us?"

"No. This is supposed to be vacation! I don't even know what we're doing here. We're supposed to be out on our boat."

That exchange ended the teachable moment, and Mickie and Lena came back to our area with a vidscreen and huddled a long time with Mrs. Veck.

My attention snapped back to reality when I heard the ambulance door slam shut. The dark boy had slipped outside. Almost immediately after, I heard a sharp, crackling sound from somewhere beneath me. What was it? Where was it coming from?

I listened for a few seconds, and I heard it again. It was close by. A new burst of sound led me toward the foot of the stretcher. I scooted forward on my hips until I could bend and look underneath.

The first thing I saw was my backpack, a familiar dark red shape against the white metal floor. It looked very flat. I wondered what the kidnappers had left inside it. The next thing I saw was the dark boy's two-way resting against a rubber wheel of the stretcher. He had, apparently, left it behind. What would Dr. Reyes think about that?

I leaned closer and listened for a moment. The crackling gave way to voices, at least two of them. They were arguing, it seemed, in a foreign language. Creole? I suspected so. Some words were clear, and they sounded like French.

I soon gave up trying to understand them and scooted back

up to my usual position. I thought for a moment about the dark boy. He presented himself as being such a genius. Had he just made a really stupid mistake? Could I, if I had the nerve, pick up that two-way and call for help? To Victoria? Or to Patience?

Most likely not. Most likely I would need a password to use it. Or maybe he had left it there on purpose to see if I could be trusted? But what if he hadn't? What if it had been pure stupidity on his part? Just a stupid, dumbass mistake. What would Dr. Reyes do to him for that? Would the dark boy get treated any better than the guy who had fallen asleep in the front cab? I didn't think so.

Anyway, my moment of opportunity soon vanished when the dark boy returned. He sat down without a glance toward me, picked up the two-way, and joined in the Creole conversation.

I sat there for a good ten minutes, mentally kicking myself, feeling myself a coward for not trying to get help on the two-way. Patience would have tried it. Most kids I know would have tried it, with the possible exception of Hopewell.

That's because most kids had never been taken. Only Hopewell and I knew what it was really like to face kidnappers; to try to remember our training; to try to survive.

So I forgave myself. I told myself that I was doing the right thing. I forced myself to concentrate again on the events of December 22.

The Highlands guard pulled the van into a church parking lot near the center of Mangrove. He let the engine idle while he contacted the local police on a securescreen.

Mangrove was an interesting place to me. It was as different from The Highlands as it could possibly be. The town had a combination of dirt roads full of deep ruts and asphalt roads full of potholes. The roads were lined on both sides with brightly colored cinder-block houses—green, pink, orange. The houses had rusty room air conditioners sticking out of the sides and ripped screen doors in front.

Something must have been wrong, because we sat at that church for a long time. While we waited, Patience and I quietly played a game called Syllogisms. It's a logic game that you can use to prove or disprove any point (naturally, we learned it from Mrs. Veck). There are different types of syllogisms to choose from. For example, the Categorical Syllogism says that everybody in a category has the same thing.

I started the game by stating the first premise: "All members of the Dugan family have coarse hairs sprouting from their noses."

Patience then stated the second premise: "Pauline is a member of the Dugan family."

I stated the conclusion: "Therefore, Pauline has coarse hairs sprouting from her nose."

Then we switched, and Patience began: "All girls who wear the same white shirt to satschool and to cheerleader practice have pit stains."

I added: "Maureen wears the same white shirt to satschool and to cheerleader practice."

Patience concluded: "Therefore, Maureen has pit stains."

I started a third one: "All mammals have spines."

Patience opened her mouth to respond; then she stopped and glared at me.

I suggested, "Hopeless does not—"

But she cut me off. "What? What are you saying? My brother doesn't have a spine?" She looked like she was about to punch me.

Patience had been getting very impatient with Hopewell jokes, especially after the attack by the Dugans. I leaned back and muttered, "Uh, sorry."

"Do you really think that? Because it's not true."

"No. I just said it for fun."

"Fun?"

"Yeah."

She continued angrily, "Fun? Really? From you? Isn't your idea of fun to follow your maid around the kitchen?"

Now I was the one who was offended, but I responded meekly: "I said I was sorry."

Patience's eyes bored into mine. "And don't call him that stupid name anymore."

"I won't. Take it easy."

"No, I won't take it easy! That's when people attack you, when you take it easy. That's why the Dugans thought they could attack Hopewell, because even *I* was going along with it. I was treating my own brother like a joke. Well, I'm not doing that anymore."

"Okay. I get it. I'm sorry."

She finally mumbled, "Okay."

After that, we sat in awkward silence until the van started to move. We left the parking lot of the church, a Catholic one called La Iglesia de la Natividad, and turned onto the main road. It was a nice wide road without any potholes. I could see a makeshift stage ahead, positioned in front of a building that said MANGROVE TOWN HALL.

Just before the van stopped for good, Albert stood up and addressed us all. "Stay within the perimeter established by Security. Speak only to the kids within that perimeter."

We parked behind a big oak tree. Mickie and her crew led the way out. They were followed by Mr. Patterson, the butlers, Mrs. Veck, the students, and the maids. The first thing I noticed was a large vidscreen, about four meters high, set up in front and to the left of the stage. The audience members would have close-up views of Mickie on that. Her rectangular red glasses would appear to be ten times their normal size; so would her mole.

Up on the stage, Mickie, Lena, Mr. Patterson, and the mayor of Mangrove had resumed an argument begun the previous year. It was like no time had elapsed. The mayor, a thin old man in a black suit, wanted to talk to Mr. Patterson on-air about starting new businesses in Mangrove. Mickie told him, "That's dead airtime, Mr. Mayor. Nobody wants to listen to that."

We students were supposed to mingle with kids from Mangrove in a loose circle in front of the stage. Our security guards and butlers flanked us on one side; several men with Town of Mangrove police uniforms flanked us on the other. Just as in the previous year, though, none of the kids really interacted, and that was too bad. I would have liked to.

Also as in the previous year, the Mangrove kids gravitated to Victoria like she was a movie star. I pointed that out to Patience: "Mickie never lets Victoria get near the camera because she's so attractive. You know? She makes Mickie look like a monkey. No offense to monkeys."

Patience smiled slightly, so I guess I was finally forgiven for mocking Hopewell. She joined me as we unloaded the bags of clothing and started passing them out to the Mangrove kids.

Kurt set up his camera to shoot the scene. Lena told the Highlands kids to "smile" and the Mangrove kids to *"sonreir."* We had soon passed out all sixteen bags of clothes. Then Lena and Mrs. Veck distributed the books—dozens and dozens of them—all describing the bilingual adventures of Ramiro Fortunato.

After that, Kurt changed position to vid the locals presenting their gifts—the homemade *tornada* dolls—to the visitors. Some of us said *"Gracias"* to the Mangrove kids. Some of us (I don't need to tell you who) laughed at them.

Maureen Dugan held her doll up and cried, "Gross! Its ears look like Hopewell's."

Pauline added, "It'd be even grosser if it looked like Sterling Johnston."

I don't think the Mangrove kids understood their comments, which was good for everyone involved.

Mrs. Veck herded us to the right side of the stage. The local kids, along with a few adults, congregated on the left side. Mickie then walked out carrying a wireless microphone. Lena pulled out a bilingual sign that read APPLAUSE/APLAUSOS and pumped it up and down until members of the audience, mostly from the Mangrove side, applauded.

Mickie gave the crowd a big smile that was almost frightening on the four-meter vidscreen. "Welcome! Welcome, all of you, to the third annual Kid-to-Kid Day. We are in the town of Mangrove, Florida. As always, I am joined by the mayor, the Honorable Samuel Ortiz. Welcome, Mr. Mayor."

Samuel Ortiz walked out slowly and stood next to her. He

leaned into the microphone. "Welcome to you, Mickie. This is actually *our* home, so I should be welcoming you."

"Thank you. Did you see that scene earlier with all those kids giving to other kids?"

"Yes, I did."

"It was very touching, and, of course, it is the essence of Kid-to-Kid Day. You have some really needy kids here, don't you?"

"Some, sure. But most have what they need."

"I think all of us can use a prayer now and again, Mr. Mayor. And my trips to Mangrove and other towns always make me think of this one: 'There but for the grace of God go I.'"

He answered defiantly: "It's not so bad being us, you know."

"No. Of course not."

"There are a lot of good people here."

"There are. Let's do some good for one of them right now, shall we? Let's change one young woman's life for the better." She looked at the audience. "What do you say?"

Lena held up the APPLAUSE/APLAUSOS sign. The Mangrove side of the crowd applauded obediently.

Mickie said, "She's an RDS cook at a large estate in Palm Beach County, and I have had the pleasure of tasting her delicious cooking firsthand. Please welcome Isabella. Isabella!"

Lena helped a young woman climb up from the crowd and stand next to Mickie. The woman looked to be about twenty-five years old. She stared hard at her own feet as Mickie continued: "I happen to know that she's a big fan of the Manor House Cookbook series, those collections of recipes from the great manor houses of England. What are some of your favorite recipes, Isabella?"

Mickie thrust the microphone under the woman's chin, forcing her to look up. She was attractive, with long features and a reddish derma, as if she were part Indian. She muttered, "Beef Wellington. Chicken cordon bleu."

"Yum. Well, the people at SatPub have heard about your cooking, and they liked what they heard. They want you to have the complete series of Manor House Cookbooks, hardbound, and here they are."

Mr. Patterson walked out, all smiles, carrying a wooden display case stocked with books. Isabella looked very excited to see it.

Mickie asked, "What do you think of that, Isabella?"

The woman could only utter, "Thank you. *Gracias.*"

Mickie continued, "But, Isabella, that's not the real reason I asked you up here today. Do you remember what you told me in the kitchen that night when I came in to pay my compliments to the chef?"

Isabella looked confused.

"Do you remember what you said?"

"No. Sorry. I am sorry."

"When I asked you what you planned to do after you retired from RDS?"

"Oh. Oh yes!"

"You said your goal was to become a professional dietitian; to work for Social Services or for the school board, helping people to be healthier by eating better."

"Yes."

Lena held up her sign again; the audience applauded enthusiastically.

"That career requires a four-year college degree, doesn't it, Isabella?"

"Yes."

"What must you study to get that degree?"

"Anatomy. Nutrition. A lot of science. A lot of math."

"The tough stuff, right?"

"Yes."

"No Water Skiing 101 for you."

"No."

"And you've been saving your RDS money to help you pursue this goal."

"Yes."

"Tell me, Isabella. What kind of grades did you get in high school? And don't fib to me, because Lena has already looked them up."

The embarrassed woman answered reluctantly, "I got all A's."

"Yes, you did."

The audience applauded again, on its own.

Mickie pressed her: "And what about your CCs? Your College Comprehensives?"

Isabella answered, "All tens."

"That's ten out of a possible ten, ladies and gentlemen!"

More applause.

"Well, I am authorized to tell you that, because of your great work and your dedication, you will be receiving a full scholarship to Nova Southeastern University from the Martin County Realtors Association."

Isabella's hands flew to her mouth, and her eyes filled with tears. Mr. Patterson handed her a rolled-up piece of paper with a gold seal on it as the Mangrove side of the audience applauded and cheered for several seconds.

When the clamor died down, Mickie gave the "cut" sign to Kurt, and Lena escorted Isabella from the stage.

As Mickie and her crew prepared for the next segment, Patience and I decided to try to mingle with the Mangrove kids. I used the Spanish I'd learned from Victoria, smiling at friendly-looking kids and saying, *"Como está?"*

When they would reply, I would answer *"Bien,"* like Victoria had taught me.

Patience giggled at my efforts.

Pauline watched us and commented, "Look at the hors. They're pretending they can speak Spanish."

Patience replied, "So? You pretend you can speak English."

Pauline sneered. "I can."

Patience muttered to me, "It's sad when they can't even fight back."

Pauline turned to Sierra. "You must know Spanish. Right?"

"Not right. I don't know any."

"Then does your dad?"

"No. Why would he?"

"Well, isn't your last name Vasquez or something?"

"Yeah. So what? Why would I want to know Spanish? You get the servants to translate for you. That's their job."

I squeezed Patience's arm secretly as I confided to them, "Personally, I would want to know what the servants were saying about me."

Sierra looked quickly at her maid. "What? What are they saying about me?"

Patience took over from there. "We heard all the maids talking about you just now, over by the van."

"What? They're not allowed to do that."

"They didn't know we were listening."

Sierra believed her. She demanded to know what they said.

Patience leaned forward. "I'm not sure. I don't know a lot of vocabulary. They either said you were *miedosa* or *mierda*."

"What do those mean?"

"One means 'scared'; the other means 'excrement.'"

As Sierra stood and contemplated that, Patience and I turned and hurried into the crowd, laughing uncontrollably.

I was still chuckling about Sierra when I got pulled back to my ambulance prison by a loud sound, the sound of the dark boy's seat snapping shut.

I said, "Hey! Are you going to the bathroom?"

He ignored me, so I added, "Because I need to go to the bathroom. That's your job, right? Helping me go to the bathroom?"

He answered angrily, "No. That is not my job. I'll get Dr. Reyes."

"No! No, please. Do me a favor, one small favor. All you have to do is take me there and bring me back."

His face twisted in disbelief. "What? Do you think I'm stupid?"

"No. Not at all. You'll be right with me, right outside the door. Come on, where am I going to go? You have me surrounded."

"No. I have to get the doctor."

"Please. Please."

He opened the ambulance door, but I called after him, "Come on! This is a better way. I know it is."

He jumped down. But then he turned around and said, "I'll talk to the doctor. Wait here for his answer."

When the door opened a minute later, I found out the answer, and it was no. Dr. Reyes himself climbed in, placed the bedpan on the stretcher, and left. All in silence.

Then he returned two minutes later to fetch it.

It was humiliating and disgusting, once again. But there was one small consolation—the dark boy had at least talked to Dr. Reyes for me.

He had done me a small favor.

Once the dark boy was back inside and seated, I asked, "How are things going?" I quickly answered myself: "They're going smoothly, I hope. Ten hours left to go. Is the ransom plan moving forward?"

I waited for a full minute for him to respond. It frightened me that he wouldn't even make eye contact. I hoped it wasn't because the plan had hit a snag. I finally looked over at my vidscreen. The red light was on. Who was watching? Was it my father? Were they in contact with my father? Were they showing him that I was still alive? For now?

Good, I thought. Let him see that I was holding up my end of the deal and that I was waiting for him to hold up his. Let him see that I was using my training. With a last look at the red light, I composed myself, closed my eyes, and concentrated . . .

The Mangrove kids and the Highlands kids returned to their respective sides of the stage as Mickie appeared again with a microphone. She leaned over and held the mike out to some brown-skinned kids. "Tell me about the *tornada* dolls. What is the story behind those?"

A tall girl—preselected, I'm sure—volunteered to answer. "You give it to someone you hope you will see again someday."

Mickie said, "That's nice." She pointed to another girl. "Wait a minute. You still have yours! Can I take a look at it?"

The girl looked away, frightened. She clearly did not want to give her doll up, but after some wrangling in Spanish with the other kids, she handed it over.

"Now, what's this carved on here? Is it the letter *L*?"

The tall girl answered for her: "It's usually the letter of a person's name. But they told us to do ours with the letter *H*."

"To stand for The Highlands?"

"That's right."

Mickie handed the doll back to the frightened girl. "Thank you, honey."

I could see on the big screen that the girl had a thin carved line across her top lip. I whispered to Patience, "Look at her mouth."

Patience knew what I meant right away. She explained, "That line is a surgical scar. She must have had a cleft palate. That's when your teeth show all the time."

"Your top lip is deformed, right?"

"Something like that. It's a birth defect. But it looks like she had hers operated on."

The segment wrapped quickly, after which the girl with the scar walked right over to us and stopped in front of Albert. Albert looked at her, then swiftly turned on his heels and slipped away. The girl seemed confused. But then she turned to Patience and me and smiled. The surgical line disappeared entirely, leaving only white teeth and brown derma.

She pointed to where Albert had been standing. "Please. *La tornada,* for him."

I took it from her. "Okay. Why for him? *Por qué?*"

The girl smiled even wider. *"Por gracias."*

"Gracias? That's it?"

She threw up her hands. "That's it."

"Okay. I'll give it to him."

Right after that, Maureen Dugan saw a Mangrove girl holding up a pair of jeans. She shouted out angrily, "Those are mine! I still wear those!" She stalked toward the bewildered girl and snatched them back. Then she spotted another pair in another girl's hand. "Those, too! Give them back!"

Pauline heard this and scanned the crowd, coming to a halt at a young girl's feet. "Who gave my flip-flops away? Those are my favorite flip-flops. I wear them every day." She rounded on her maid, a dark-haired, sharp-featured woman from Romania. "Colette! Who gave those away? Was it you?"

"No, Miss Pauline. It was your mother."

"My mother? What is she, stupid?"

Colette didn't answer, so Pauline prodded her. "Well?"

"I . . . I don't know, Miss."

Other Mangrove kids gathered quickly behind the young girl. Two groups were now facing off.

Another Mangrove girl stepped forward and flung a white shirt at Maureen Dugan's face. "Here. Keep this. It's got pit stains anyway."

Maureen pulled the shirt away from her face and shook her head back and forth, totally flustered. But Pauline was not flustered. She stepped up and flung her wooden doll at the

71

girl, catching her right on the cheek. "Here! You can keep this! It was going in the garbage anyway."

I looked over at the group of adults posing in front of Kurt the cameraman. Mickie was speaking to the mayor while Mr. Patterson, Mrs. Veck, and a group of people from the town looked on. They were completely unaware that the whole "kid-to-kid" scene, just ten meters away from them, was unraveling in a very ugly way.

A boy started yelling at Sterling Johnston, "Get away from my sister, you sick freak!" Sterling backed away slowly, which only drew more attention to him.

Another group of boys started in on Hopewell, haranguing him in Spanish and making little slapping motions at his face. Hopewell tried to backpedal, but he lost his balance and fell on the asphalt, skinning his elbow.

Patience and I hurried over to help him up, but Albert and James got there first. The Mangrove boys backed away as soon as the men intervened. Albert shouted at me, "Miss Charity! All of you! Get in the security van. Right now!"

Patience and I made a quick about-face and hurried toward the van. I watched one Highlands guard jump into the driver's seat while the other pulled the machine gun out of its rack. I turned and saw that James had pulled Hopewell to his feet and was fast-walking him toward us.

Suddenly all of the butlers were involved. Albert, William, and Edward formed a line behind Hopewell. Each had a can of biorepellent out and was brandishing it at the Mangrove kids. This just seemed to make the kids angrier.

Patience and I hurried up the van steps, followed by Sierra, the Dugans, the four maids, and Sterling Johnston.

Hopewell and the four butlers climbed on right after. The guards closed the steel doors and glared at the mob through the tinted windows.

The Mangrove kids retreated behind a tree. They started talking among themselves in an animated way and making violent gestures.

About one minute later, Mickie Meyers wrapped up her shoot and returned to the van with Mrs. Veck, Mr. Patterson, Lena, and Kurt, walking right past the roiling mob.

They had no idea what had just happened. They had no idea, that is, until the van pulled away and we all heard the thuds. Objects started crashing against the windows. I pressed my face against a tinted window and saw what the objects were—Ramiro Fortunato novels, dozens and dozens of them—all hurled at us angrily by the children of Mangrove.

Mickie finally looked up and inquired, of no one in particular, "Why are they doing that?" No one volunteered an answer, so she let the matter drop.

The van roared away as fast as the driver could go, not stopping until we reached a turnpike rest area. The driver swerved into it and pulled to a halt in front of the food court. Both guards then stepped outside. One held the machine gun at a downward angle while the other circumnavigated the van, looking for damage.

Albert took a seat next to Hopewell and examined his bleeding elbow. He pulled out a small first-aid kit and started to clean the wound.

As she watched Albert in action, Patience said, "Remember the girl with the cleft palate?"

"Yeah."

"She looked really good. Better than Hopewell, you know?"

"Yeah."

"I wonder who did the surgery."

"A clinic doctor?"

"No way. She'd look mangled."

"Then a real doctor, I guess."

Albert finished bandaging Hopewell's elbow and was coming back up the aisle. Patience told him, "You're really good at medical stuff, Albert. You should be a clinic doctor."

Albert smiled. "Thank you, Miss Patience."

"Would you like to do that?"

"No. I'm happy doing what I do." He kept walking up to his seat.

Patience asked Daphne, "What do you have to do to be a clinic doctor?"

"I don't think you have to do anything," Daphne answered. "You rent a house or a storefront, put up a sign, and start calling yourself a doctor."

Patience wrinkled her nose. "That's it? Anyone who wants to call himself, or herself, a doctor can set up a clinic?"

"Pretty much."

"You don't need to go to medical school?"

"No. I suppose you could, but there's nobody to check if you did or did not. You can print yourself a phony diploma, buy a pack of tongue depressors, and start telling people to say *Ahh*."

Just then, Mickie and Kurt came down the aisle and set up in front of Mrs. Veck. Mickie explained, "We were looking at the tapes from before. I want to hear a little more about something that you said."

The red light on Kurt's camera came on. Mickie smiled into it. "Mrs. Veck, you used a phrase before that I had never heard, so I wrote it down: 'rituals of social inversion.' Can you tell me a little more about those?"

Mrs. Veck smiled. "Certainly. What would you like to know?"

"Well, you gave a very interesting example about the Three Kings bowing down to the baby Jesus. You're saying that's an 'inversion' because you'd expect the opposite to happen, right?"

"Right."

"What are some more examples of inversions?"

"Shall we see if the students can think of any?"

Mickie shook her head. "No. Just give me a few yourself."

"All right. Well, I remember one that had to do with boy chimney sweeps in London, back in Victorian times."

"Excellent."

"They worked at a dirty, dangerous job, and their faces were always black from it. But on one day of the year, they would paint their faces white and have a grand parade. The people would honor them on that one day; then the boys would go back to their black faces for the other three hundred sixty-four days."

"Interesting. Any others?"

"Yes. There's a very famous one that has survived over the years—April Fools' Day. On that day, the most dishonored person in society, the fool, was honored by everyone else. Then he went back to being the fool."

"That was a real inversion."

"It was."

"Now, why did the Victorians have these rituals?"

"I believe it was part of the social contract in Victorian times. The poor people had to be part of society; otherwise society wouldn't work. The poor might decide to rise up and attack the rich! Through these rituals, the poor agreed to an exchange. They would be on top of society for one day, and then they would be on the bottom for the other three hundred sixty-four."

Patience muttered to me the exact word that I was thinking: "Fools."

Back at The Highlands, the security van dropped us all off at our respective houses. Patience got off with me, though, along with Victoria, Albert, Mickie, Lena, and Kurt.

My father was waiting there in the front yard, holding a controller in both hands. He was playing with the helicopter drone, making it rise and land by remote control. Without actually looking at me, he called out, "What are you up to?"

"We had a school field trip."

"Oh? Where'd you go?"

"Mangrove. For Kid-to-Kid Day."

"Uh-huh. Listen, honey, I have to talk to Albert for a minute. Okay?"

"Sure."

He winked conspiratorially. "I've got the college bowl season coming up. Gotta get him to check out the weather alerts for me."

"Okay."

"Gotta get my flight plans squared away this time, too, or the FAA will get mad."

I just shrugged and continued inside, but I muttered to

Patience, "Gee, Dad, I did have a thing or two more to say. We did have some trouble down there, but we managed to escape with our lives. Thank you for asking."

Patience and I then sat in my room for two hours. We spent most of that time analyzing the boys from the Amsterdam Academy satschool. We criticized some, assigning them names like Mr. I'm Too Cool to Look at the Camera and Mr. My Mother Dresses Me Funny. We drooled over others, and plotted how we might meet them in person. Or "in the flesh," as Patience put it, which I told her was "a very horish thing to say."

At 17:00, Herbert, the Pattersons' butler, arrived to drive Patience home for dinner. I walked her as far as the wrought-iron gate. Then I walked back inside and sat in the dining room. Victoria had prepared beef Wellington with Yorkshire pudding, a favorite dish of mine from *The Manor House Book of Festive Recipes*. My father, my ex-stepmother, and I consumed the food as unfestively as possible, just sitting there and chewing silently, like three strangers.

Dessalines

There was another type of syllogism that Patience and I used in our game. The Disjunctive Syllogism says that something either *is* or *is not*. I decided to try it by myself.

My first premise was: The dark boy is either evil or good. My second premise was: The dark boy is not evil (because he tried to get me out of that last bedpan thing). Therefore, my conclusion had to be: The dark boy is good. Or at least he has some good in him.

I believed that he did. I believed it enough to try to talk to him. First, as a show of good faith, I reached over, grabbed the bottle of SmartWater, and took a swig. I waited for a positive reaction, or any reaction at all, from him, but none came. I finally muttered, "Excuse me. Excuse me. You know my name, but I don't know yours."

He looked up from the two-way, but not really at me.

"I need a name for you. I need something to call you."

He turned toward me slowly and answered, "What kind of fool do you think I am? I'm not telling you my name."

"It doesn't have to be your *real* name. It can be anything. Like you guys call each other names — Monnonk, and stuff."

His eyes registered surprise, like he had been caught off guard. "We do?"

"Yeah. I hear you."

"Okay. Well, *don't* hear us. You might hear the wrong thing; then you'd be in danger."

"Oh? Like I'm not now?"

He shook his head. "You're safe enough, as long as you listen. So *taissez-vous, et écoutez*."

"What's that?"

"Be quiet and listen."

"All right. But when I do need to . . . address you, what do I say? It's disrespectful to just start talking to someone."

He looked at me curiously, like he thought I might be mocking him. "Disrespectful?"

"Yes."

"*Alors.* I'll tell you what. You can call me a name. You can call me Dessi."

"Dezi?"

He rolled his eyes. "No. Not 'Dezi' with a z. Not like some *I Love Lucy* Ricky Ricardo Seventy-fifth Anniversary Vidcelebration. No! It's *Dessi*. With an s. It stands for Dessalines."

He challenged me. "Do you know who that was?"

"No."

"Do you want to?"

"Yes."

"Jean Jacques Dessalines was a hero in Haiti. He drove the French out in 1803. He massacred the whites and made himself the emperor. He won a great victory for the slaves."

"So Dessalines was a hero to the Haitian people?"

"Yes. He still is."

"Okay. So I'll call you Dessi."

He turned back to his two-way. I looked at the vidscreen clock: it was 15:17. I said, "Excuse me again. But how is the plan going? Does everybody know what to do . . . with the ransom and everything?"

"I don't know."

"Isn't that the plan?"

"I guess so. I don't really know."

I felt a sudden chill. "Has something gone wrong?"

"No."

I swallowed hard; then I asked him what I really wanted to know. "Did anybody get hurt?"

"Hurt? Who?"

"Albert. My butler."

His skin seemed to redden. "Uh, I don't know. You don't need to know, either."

I gritted my teeth. I balled up my fists and pressed them down into the stretcher. I wanted to shout at him, "I already know! You killed him! He was my armed guard, so you killed him!" But I didn't. With a great effort, I forced thoughts of Albert out of my mind so I could ask, as calmly as I could, "And what about Victoria? What happened to her?"

Dessi replied, "Let's focus on what's going to happen to you."

"If you hurt Victoria—"

"No one hurt Victoria."

"Why should I believe that?"

"Because it was not necessary to hurt her. No one did anything that was not necessary."

"Oh? And Albert? Was it necessary to kill him?"

"I did not kill anybody."

"Then Dr. Reyes, or one of the others?"

He stood up. I could tell he was getting flustered. "I can't talk about this."

I pressed him, "Please. You have to understand: I am a human being. So is Albert. We are real people, just like you."

He shook his head adamantly. "This conversation is over."

I pushed myself forward on the stretcher, right to the edge, as if I might jump off. He raised his hands to stop me. I shouted, "Please, just tell me. Is my Albert dead?"

He glared at me for about fifteen seconds. Then, in an icy voice, he whispered, "Yes. He is. He is dead."

I sat in stunned silence for a moment; then I leaned back on the stretcher, sick to my soul. I felt like I was in a night terror, but it was real. Way too real. How could this be? How could anything change so absolutely, so totally, just like that? How could Albert, so strong and alive, be dead just like that?

Suddenly I felt like I had to vomit. I felt my throat open up all the way down to my stomach. But there was nothing in there to come up, just stale air in a disgusting dry heave. I flipped over on the stretcher and buried my face in the sheet.

With a great effort of will, I forced myself to block out all evil thoughts. I forced myself to travel somewhere else, to a safer place. Where? Anywhere. To The Highlands. To Christmas Eve. To a living memory of Albert.

I remembered Albert sitting in the kitchen. I was watching him through a crack in the door. He was at the breakfast counter, playing with his small leather chess set. Albert played with that chess set a lot. Patience told me that Herbert had told her that he was very good. I don't know. I never played with him; that was against regulations.

Victoria was stringing a long garland made from many different kinds of nuts. I was eager to help with it, but I had to wait until Albert left the kitchen. He disapproved of me helping with any of the housework, or learning Spanish, or fraternizing in any way with Victoria.

That's why I was standing at the door—waiting, peeking, eavesdropping. I didn't often do that. RDS servants are so well trained that it's usually not worth it. They never talk about anything interesting, or personal, or unprofessional. That's why I was surprised to hear Albert saying, "So how do you feel about that? I mean, personally?"

The conversation had obviously been going on for a while, because Victoria's voice sounded weary. "I already told you how I feel about it."

"No, you didn't. You said it didn't affect you. That's not true. How could it not affect you?"

"I meant . . . I don't need to talk about it. It didn't affect me like that, like I need to talk about it."

After a pause, he continued: "But you *should* talk about it."

Victoria had heard enough. "I want to talk about other things now. Like how we're going to serve the dinner tonight. Like how we're going to finish all these decorations in time. Like how the family will exchange gifts."

After a loud sigh, Albert observed, "I didn't see any gifts out there."

"They're going to put some gifts in the stockings."

"If they are, it'll just be currency. Or gift certificates."

"There's nothing wrong with that."

"Personally, I prefer real gifts."

"People can buy whatever they want with currency. Currency is practical."

"Have Mr. or Ms. Meyers been to the vault today to get currency?"

"I don't know." Victoria's voice dropped as she added, "It's really not my job to know."

Their conversation died out after that, so I made some shuffling sounds with my feet and then opened the door.

Victoria smiled her dazzling smile. "Hello, Miss. *Feliz Navidad.*"

"*Feliz Navidad.*"

"*Gracias.* Are you ready for Christmas Eve?"

"Sure."

Albert nodded. "Hello, Miss Charity."

"Hello, Albert. Merry Christmas."

"Merry Christmas."

I played dumb. "Did either of you see where my parents hid my gifts?"

Albert shook his head. "You know we are sworn not to tell things like that."

"I know. I was just wondering. I hope they're not giving me anything stupid, like a Miami Hurricanes jersey."

Victoria asked, "What do you want?"

"I don't know. Something practical."

Albert shot me a quick look, like he knew I had been listening. He put away his chess pieces, folded up the leather case, and stood up. "I'd better decorate that living room."

As soon as the door closed behind him, Victoria said, "Why aren't you out with a friend, having a great adventure?"

This was another of her not-so-casual questions. She was always on me about not going out, having fun, living my life. I answered, "Patience can't come over. Her grandparents are visiting until fourteen-thirty."

"Then what about someone else?"

"Who?"

"Someone on-screen, maybe? You could play a game. Someone from the Amsterdam Academy?"

"Who?"

Victoria gave up on that tack and tried, "Well, then, what about doing something on your own? Something adventurous, something thrilling."

"What?"

"There are many activities for young people in The Highlands."

"You sound like the real estate brochure."

Victoria smiled and continued: "Many safe, supervised, yet still thrilling activities."

"Right. Maybe I could go water-skiing with Albert and the guards, maybe out on the canal or on Killer Bass Lake. I could have four of them around me, with their Glocks, in a diamond formation. You know? Like in a water-skiing show?"

Victoria tried hard to keep a straight face, but she lost the struggle and burst out laughing.

I threw up my arms. "Oh, the thrill of it all!"

When she regained her composure, she finally stated the obvious: "You've come to help me make decorations, haven't you?"

"Yes, please. What are you making?"

Victoria picked up a long sheet of paper. "Let's see what I am making. Project one: a Victorian nut garland to drape across the mantel of the fireplace, composed of pinecones, Brazil nuts, walnuts, almonds, chicken wire, and moss. Project two: red- and blue-velvet stockings to be hung over the fireplace, one for each family member, decorated with tartan plaid trim. Project three: strings of Edwardian Christmas cards hanging from gold and green ribbons."

She looked at me. "Pick your project."

"I'll help make the stockings."

"All right." Victoria rummaged in the pantry and pulled out a box. It contained scissors, thread, and different colors of velvet. "Here. We're using last year's stockings, but we're adding new trim." She reached down and pulled up three stockings. One said *Charity;* one said *Hank;* one said *Mickie.* I set to work cutting and adding trim to them while Victoria finished the nut garland.

I asked, "How do you say 'stockings'?"

Victoria checked to see if Albert was near, then whispered, *"Medias."*

"What about 'Christmas stockings'?"

"Medias de Navidad."

"That makes sense."

After two minutes of silent work, Victoria commented, "Do you know who always gives practical gifts?"

"Who?"

"Ramiro Fortunato."

"I remember."

"Yes. He does not waste his money on silly, useless gifts that people don't want. Instead, he buys his mother a new, more powerful vacuum for her housecleaning business. He buys his father a new set of socket wrenches for his auto-repair business."

"What's he doing in his latest adventure? Is he still mowing lawns?"

By way of reply, she reached into another box and pulled out a paperback book. "No more lawn business. He has joined the marines, for five years." She handed the book to me to examine. "Then he is going to go to college, on a full scholarship."

"Good for him."

"Yes. He is brave, hardworking, and practical."

"You really should marry him, Victoria."

"I will. You wait and see."

I laughed. "Maybe I will, too."

She warned me playfully, "No, you stay away from my Ramiro."

I studied the front and back covers and flipped through the pages. "What do you like best about these books?"

Victoria's mouth dropped open, as if she couldn't believe the question. "What do I like best? I like everything! For Ramiro, every day is a great adventure. And do you know why?"

"Why?"

She stretched her arms wide. "Simply because he is open to having adventures."

I handed the book back. "That's because he doesn't live in The Highlands."

She smiled curiously, like she does when she's studying me. "You mean, like you?"

"Yeah."

"You mean sometimes you feel lonely here?"

"Oh yeah."

Victoria told me, firmly but kindly, "Part of that is in your head, Miss Charity. Part of that is because you stay closed up in the house." I started to protest, but she talked over me. "You need to be more like Ramiro: more open to life, to the wondrous thrill of living."

"In The Highlands? Come on. I'm surrounded by security."

She looked out the window. "It is difficult now, yes. But maybe when you are a little older, when you are out in the world . . ."

I conceded, "Yeah, okay—maybe then," and went back to work.

Just as I was finishing my third stocking, Albert came back in and took hold of the enormous nut garland. He looked at my scissors disapprovingly. Then he asked Victoria, "What's the final count for dinner?"

"Seven. Mr. and Ms. Meyers; Mr. and Mrs. Patterson; Miss Charity; Miss Patience; Mr. Hopewell."

"All right. I'll hang this up. Then I'll do the place settings."

"Thank you."

Albert exited, carrying the nut garland around his neck like an engorged python.

I handed the box of materials back to Victoria and asked, "What's on the menu?"

Victoria laughed. "It is 'a cornucopia of delights.' Or at least that's what it says in this cookbook." She pointed to an open copy of *The Manor House Christmas Cookbook*. "You will be trying many new, or I should say many old, dishes for your Christmas Eve celebration."

"Let me guess. Foods from the Edwardian era."

"That's exactly right."

"I heard that King Edward was a fat pig. *Un puerco gordo.*"

Victoria sputtered a laugh and said, "Good Spanish."

"I'm serious. He was a county-fair prize hog, like a hundred and fifty kilograms."

"Well, we're cooking healthy versions of the foods tonight. I hope you will enjoy them. And the games."

"Oh no! Not games!"

"Oh yes."

I trudged toward the door in despair. "Edwardian-era decorations, foods, and games. This dinner is a Mickie Meyers vidspecial, isn't it?"

Victoria shrugged politely.

I left the kitchen, muttering to myself, "Of course it is. What isn't?"

I must have nodded off on my stretcher because, incredibly, I looked at the vidscreen clock and it was 16:20. I was shocked!

I never fall asleep without really trying to. Never. Sleeping has always been difficult for me. Was it something in the SmartWater? Or was I just exhausted?

I had a few seconds of peace before the awful memory of Albert's death returned. My eyes welled up with tears, and I cried silently for a long minute. Then, all on its own, the voice of my Highlands training returned. It whispered inside my head, telling me what I had to do: I had to accept the un-acceptable, Albert's murder. I had to accept it temporarily anyway, in order to survive. Afterward, once I got back home, I would avenge him. I swore I would. If the police wouldn't do it, then Patience and I would do it ourselves. We would hunt Dr. Reyes down with a Glock and fill him full of bullets. We would. Albert would be avenged.

For the time being, though, I had to control myself. I had to cooperate with my part in the plan. I sat up and looked at Dessi. He wasn't staring at the two-way anymore; he was reading a book. A glance at the cover told me what it was. Before I'd left for "the hospital," Victoria told Albert to put a book in my backpack. I hadn't thought about it again until that moment.

I was upset that Dessi had gone through my stuff, but not surprised. I'm sure the kidnappers had gone through all of my belongings, looking for anything dangerous to their plan, any-thing that might lead to them getting caught.

When he saw me looking at him, Dessi just held the book up distastefully, like it was a smelly sock. He asked, "What is this?"

"What? You don't know the Ramiro Fortunato books?"

"No. Do you read these?"

"Yeah. Why?"

"Why? They look like they're for first graders."

"No, they don't. They're bilingual books. People read them to learn Spanish. Or English."

"Then they don't work very well."

"What do you mean?"

He sneered. "Do you speak Spanish?"

"Yes. I know quite a bit."

"Like what?"

"Like I can speak it when I want to."

"Say something for me. Say one word."

"Okay. *Mierda.*"

Dessi smiled. "Yeah. I know that one. Kids always learn the dirty words first. In French, it's *merde.*"

Dessi turned toward me and read from the back cover of the book, his lip curling higher and higher: "Ramiro Fortunato won the school spelling bee. He led his soccer team to the state championship. Ramiro Fortunato only got into one fight—with a drug dealer—and he drove him away from the school. He started his own lawn business. Once he saw a lawn guy across the street steal from a garage." He looked up at me. "I bet it was a black guy."

"No. I remember that book, and it wasn't."

"Really? I'll have to take your word for that."

"It wouldn't hurt you to read one."

"I think it might."

"Reading's good for you."

"Hey. I read. I read real books. These do not qualify as real books."

"Oh? Then what are they?"

He shook the book at me. "They are social engineering. They are telling someone like me how to behave, how to be a good boy. And they double nicely as military recruiting. This fine young man joined the marines, right?"

"I believe he did. What's wrong with that?"

"Nothing. I'm glad he did. Now maybe they'll leave me alone."

"You could do worse than be like Ramiro Fortunato. He's a hero."

"He's not a hero! He's not anything. He doesn't even exist. He is a fictional character invented by the masters to keep the slaves in their place."

"I see. So who's your hero? That Dessalines?"

"*Oui*. Dessalines was born a slave, but he did not die one. He died an emperor."

"So is that what you want to be, too?"

"An emperor? No."

"What, then?"

"A doctor."

I could tell that he was serious now, so I tried to keep him talking. "Why?"

"Why?" He stared right into my eyes. "Because my mother needed a doctor once, but she couldn't get one."

"Why was that?"

"Because she didn't have a health-care plan. And she didn't have currency."

"Well, couldn't you have taken her to—"

He cut me off roughly. "No! You don't know anything about her!" He stood up, suddenly agitated. "I will be back in five minutes. You stay where you are. Others are watching the

91

ambulance. Several others. You are not to get off that stretcher for any reason."

He threw the door open, jumped down, and slammed it shut.

I looked at the vidscreen. Not surprisingly, the red light was on. The time was now 16:31. A little over seven hours to go. Why weren't we moving on to the next step in the plan? Why hadn't I heard anything about the ransom drop or about the plan to release me? Was there a problem?

Of course there was a problem! I knew what it was, and I knew who it was. My father. He was the problem. Maybe they couldn't reach him. Maybe he had disappeared with one of his football buddies and he wasn't answering his phone. Or worse, maybe they *had* reached him but he was stalling, or negotiating, or making some other stupid mistake that you are never, ever supposed to do with kidnappers. They wouldn't tolerate that. They would move right to the next step, the step where they cut off a part of my body looking for the GTD and send it to him to get him to shut his stupid mouth and bring the currency. That stupid man! Playing with his stupid toys! Living it up, enjoying his selfish, thoughtless, stupid life!

Somebody had to wake him up.

Well, I hadn't lived with Mickie Meyers for three years for nothing. I leaned forward and stared into the red light. I delivered a powerful video performance, a performance worth broadcasting to my father. Through dry lips, with a cracking voice, I whispered, "Please. Help me. Do whatever it takes, Daddy. Do whatever they say to do. Help me."

I tried to squeeze out a tear, but I was too dehydrated.

The speech would have to do. My fate was in my father's hands. He had better have been listening. He had better cooperate.

For my part, all I could do was continue to be someplace else in my mind.

Foods, Drinks, and Games

As always, Victoria and Albert had decorated the house beautifully for the holidays. Albert had volunteered to help redecorate the Square, too. Perhaps he felt partially responsible for the mess. That would have been just like him.

Anyway, the damage from my father's helicopter assault had all been undone. The circle of trees, one for each of the Twelve Days of Christmas, had been restored. Santa and his reindeer had been raised from the dead. All was in order.

The "celebration" began when our group—my father, Mickie, Lena, Kurt, and I—met up with Mr. and Mrs. Patterson, Patience, and Hopewell in front of the Eight-Maids-a-Milking tree. We stood in the Square with about one hundred other Highlands residents to experience Christmas songs by the Dickens Carolers and another shower of fake snow, this time courtesy of the Martin County Fire Department.

This fake snow was actually freezing slush, expelled from fire hoses atop a hook and ladder truck. The firefighters then proceeded to spread a thin layer of slippery wetness over the streets of The Highlands. As part of the celebration, several families had modified their golf carts into sleighs in order to enjoy a "jingling sleigh ride" home.

While the rest of us were climbing into the Pattersons' sleigh, Mr. Patterson pulled my father aside and made another offer for our house. Right then and there. "I'll give you hard currency," he told him. "You can have it all in yuan if you like. I've got it right in the vault."

My father just smiled. Mickie, however, looked interested.

Patience and I climbed into the back of the sleigh last, and then it took off. The Pattersons' RDS servants, Daphne and Herbert, were left to walk behind us, traversing the slushy streets as best they could. As soon as we picked up speed, Patience whispered something very disturbing to me: "Listen to this—Daphne told Herbert that Victoria's little break in November was an emergency trip to bury her father down in Mexico City."

My eyes started to tear up immediately. I whispered, "Oh my God. No." I thought back to earlier in the day. I told her, "Albert was trying to talk to Victoria about something, but she wouldn't answer him. That must have been it." I shook my head slowly. "Why wouldn't she tell me?"

"She's not allowed. She can't tell you anything personal."

"But this is different."

Patience just shrugged. "Not really."

That made me angry. "Yes, really!"

Patience pointed to her servants. "Be careful. They're getting too close. They'll hear us." She raised her voice and changed the subject. "So, what's the theme of the show tonight?"

I was still angry, and hurt, and upset, but I managed to suppress it all. I answered, "We have two themes tonight. The dinner theme is 'An Edwardian Christmas.' "

Patience deadpanned, "There's a surprise."

"And the overall theme is 'Living with Divorce.' Mickie is doing a series on how a divorced couple can still have a good time with their kids over the holidays by agreeing not to bring up marital issues."

"That should be nice and tense."

"Do you think?"

The sleigh skidded to a halt at the front gate and we all climbed out. Mickie led everyone into the house, past the glittering white lights framing our doorway and into the sumptuously decorated foyer.

Kurt hefted a camera onto his shoulder and spun in slow circles, shooting as Mickie pointed out the different features—the nut garland, the cards on ribbons, the candles, the boughs and wreaths. After she recorded a voice-over, we all entered the dining room and found our hand-calligraphed name cards.

My father walked up to Mickie and said, "This is taking 'relentless' to a new level, isn't it?"

Mickie acted like she wasn't really listening. "What's that?"

"You're shooting our Christmas dinner now? Is nothing off-limits to you?"

Mickie settled into her seat at the head of the table. She answered coolly, "Kurt is going to shoot some footage, but I don't know how we'll use it. We'll have to see how it all goes — the foods, the drinks, the games, the readings. Maybe we'll use it next year as a Christmas special. Why? Do you object to the crew being here?"

Kurt set up a tripod across from Mickie and started vidding.

My father ignored the red light. "No. I'm glad you're making your own money."

Mickie smiled tightly. "I've always made my own money."

"But you don't always spend your own money, do you?"

Mickie, to my amazement, worked this into the show: "It is neither the time nor the place for this discussion." She looked at the camera. "Not if you're Living with Divorce for the holidays. Hello, everyone. Tonight we have friends over, including Charity's friends Patience and Hopewell. It's important to include the children's friends so that they can have their own fun.

"We will all be enjoying a traditional Edwardian Christmas celebration tonight. The menu items, all delicious, come from authentic nineteenth-century recipes. Those will be followed by some hilarious parlor games favored by King Edward, who was Queen Victoria's son.

"Then we will gather in front of the fireplace for some Christmas readings by some of the greatest nineteenth-century writers, including Robert Louis Stevenson, Leo Tolstoy, and of course Charles Dickens."

Mr. and Mrs. Patterson were already exchanging glances, perhaps wondering what they had gotten themselves into.

Mickie's voice turned solemn. "But before we eat, I'd like

to begin with Jesus' words, words we shared with the people of Mangrove last week." She raised her glass. "There but for the grace of God go I."

Mickie was certainly fond of that expression. She had used it during the Thanksgiving show, too. I think it had secretly rankled Mrs. Veck, because Mrs. Veck had given me an extra-credit assignment to look it up. I decided to share the results of that assignment with Mickie and the group. "Excuse me. Actually, that wasn't Jesus."

Mickie stared at me blankly. She finally said, "No? Are you sure?"

Patience started giggling.

I replied, "I am totally, A-plus sure."

"Who was it, then, honey?"

"It was an English preacher named John Bradford."

Mickie replied like he was some third-rate local vidshow host: "Never heard of him."

"He got burned at the stake by Bloody Mary."

My father sat up, his eyes darting between Mickie and me. He joined in on the teachable moment. "I've heard of her. Now, which queen was she? Is she related to William?"

"No. She was a Tudor. Mary Tudor. She was the daughter of Henry the Eighth."

He laughed. "Like father, like daughter!"

I had to set him straight, too (courtesy of Mrs. Veck). "No, actually, she was nothing like him. She hated her father and his Protestant church. She restored the Catholic church to power in a very bloody way."

My father nodded respectfully. "I see. Hence the name."

Mickie concluded, "Well, that's all very interesting. But

the quote is certainly appropriate for Christmas, a time when we think of the less fortunate. So I say again: 'There but for the grace of God go I.'" She raised her wineglass and held it up until the other adults did, too. Then they all drank.

Patience muttered, "In Mangrove, they probably say that about us."

Albert served another round of wine to the adults. My father chugged his in one gulp and protested playfully, "Hey! You skipped me!" Albert smiled and refilled his glass.

Mickie commented, "Yes, and it wouldn't be an Edwardian Christmas without a drunken king, would it?"

Soon Albert, with Herbert's help, started to serve the ten courses that Victoria had prepared. Mickie said to Patience and me, "Please rate the different foods for me, girls. You, too, Hopewell. I want to have the young persons' opinion."

She may have regretted that request.

Victoria was a wonderful cook, but we had no use at all for the foods from the Edwardian era, and we said so as descriptively as we could.

The mince pies were "slimy-gross."

The vegetable parcels were "vomit-inducing gross."

The "Stilton rarebit" was "throw-up-on-toast gross."

My father, at least, found our opinions amusing. He laughed at every one. And drank more wine. After the black bun, some sort of fruitcake that we agreed was "we-wouldn't-put-that-in-our-mouths gross," he announced to the group, "Charity never cared much for food." He turned to me. "Remember when I was making ElectroPlus?"

I did, but just barely. I nodded.

Mr. Patterson asked, "What's that?"

"It's an energy drink that I invented, back when I was an inventor. It was like SmartWater, but without the caffeine. It could have gone global, too. But the University of Florida threatened to sue me over the patent, so I had to give it up."

"Why? It was too much like their Gator drinks?"

"Exactly. Or so they claimed. So Charity was my first and only customer."

I remembered more. I said, "There were different colors and flavors, right?"

He laughed delightedly. "Right. Six of them. For total daily nutrition. You were supposed to drink the six flavors, one at a time, at two-hour intervals. And it worked! You drank them and you remained very healthy. But then your mother got upset. She made you go back to solid foods."

"Yeah. Yeah, I remember."

My father extended his hands to include the Pattersons. "Forgive me for saying this in the middle of dinner, or at whatever stage we are in this monumental meal, but ElectroPlus also eliminated all solid wastes from daily life. Think of that. A feces-free existence!"

Patience burst out laughing; I think Hopewell smiled a little, too. But Mr. and Mrs. Patterson shifted uncomfortably and looked at their laps. Mickie did not react at all. I'm sure she considered the entire exchange to be dead airtime, but she let Kurt keep shooting and the meal went on.

After the final course, a deadly concoction called "gilded Christmas pudding," which Patience pronounced "fresh-from-a-landfill gross," my father proposed a toast of his own. He raised his glass, waited for everyone's attention, and then announced, *"Feliz Navidad."*

Mr. Patterson asked, "Do you speak Spanish, Hank?"

"Sure. A little. I grew up in Miami."

Mrs. Patterson looked amazed. "I grew up there, too. What part?"

"Kendall."

"We were in Miami Shores."

"Miami Shores isn't as bad as Kendall, but it's still pretty bad. Have you been back there lately?"

Mrs. Patterson looked at her husband. She answered emphatically, "Oh no. Roy drove us down there about ten years ago. I wanted to show the children the house I grew up in. I couldn't believe it. The street looked like something you'd see in a war movie. We never even stopped the car."

My dad pointed to Albert and Herbert. "I wouldn't go back to my street today without these guys and an armored van. But still, in the spirit of the holiday, *La Natividad,* let's all raise up our glasses."

Everyone around the table raised a glass—some up high, like Patience and me; some barely off the table, like Mickie. My father repeated *"Feliz Navidad,"* and we all drank. Albert stepped forward to fill Dad's glass. Then Dad continued, "Okay. Now we need a new toast." He turned to Mickie. "See if you can guess who said this: 'The rendering of useful service is the common duty of mankind.' "

Mickie shrugged. "Abraham Lincoln?"

"No. Here's the next part of it: 'And only in the purifying fire of sacrifice is the dross of selfishness consumed' "—he shot a glance at me—" 'and the greatness of the human soul set free.' "

Mickie stared at him impassively. She wasn't about to try another guess.

He smiled at her. "Let me give you a hint: You were in New York, vidding the lighting of a big Christmas tree. I was just standing there, reading this quote off a wall."

Mickie's eyes widened behind her red frames. She answered, "Rockefeller Center!"

"Right you are. And the words are from . . . ?"

Mickie shook her head in quick little motions, like a metronome. "I have no idea."

"Well, the words are from John D. Rockefeller, Junior."

Nobody said anything for a moment. Mr. Patterson broke the silence by asking, "Where did his money come from, Hank? New York real estate?"

"No. Oil. Standard Oil. Which you and I still consume robustly in our big diesel cars."

Herbert entered, carrying a tray of coffee cups. He was followed immediately by Albert, carrying a pair of porcelain pitchers. They served coffee to the adults (except for my father, who waved his away) and hot chocolate to the kids.

Mrs. Patterson turned to Mickie and changed the subject. "What are you up to for the holidays, Mickie? Are you doing any shows?"

Mickie gestured toward Lena and Kurt. "We're doing two shows over the holidays, a week apart. We'll be at Disney World tomorrow for the Christmas parade."

"That's a great parade."

"We're flying to Orlando for that. Then we're flying to New York to do the New Year's Eve show in Times Square."

"Oh, I love that show."

"It'll be great this year. Lots of exciting guests."

Mrs. Patterson then turned to my father. "And how about you, Hank?"

"Ah well, it's the college football bowl season. The biggest week of the year. I'm flying to the SatPub Bowl tomorrow—Florida versus Texas."

"Tomorrow?"

"Oh yes."

"And what about for New Year's?"

"For New Year's Eve, I have the Orange Bowl Fest down in Miami. That's a great party. Then, on January first, it's football all day: the Cotton Bowl at eleven hundred hours, the Fiesta Bowl at sixteen hundred, and the Orange Bowl at twenty hundred. By twenty-three hundred hours, the Hurricanes will have been crowned the national champions."

Mrs. Patterson wagged her finger at him like he was being naughty. "Hank, what on earth do you do when there's no football?"

He held up a finger of his own. "Ah! That's easy. Golf! There's always golf."

Mr. Patterson confirmed this: "That's true. I play golf with clients all year round. Say, Hank, who's that new guy who's tearing up the junior tour?"

Dad looked bewildered. "Who?"

"That young guy. He's on all the vidscreens."

"You're gonna have to give me more to go on than that."

"The one who's winning all the tournaments!"

My father shook his head. "There are a lot of young golfers winning a lot of tournaments."

Somewhere around there is where I tuned them out. I had heard enough about my parents and their plans for the holidays. Especially since I wasn't included in any of them.

Someone knocked softly on the back of the ambulance. Dessi opened the door a crack. He reached outside and then pulled in two white shopping bags from a store named WorldMart. He opened the fatter of the two bags and dumped out a bundle of clothing that, when untangled, turned out to be a complete outfit for me—jeans, sneakers, a blue T-shirt, a black sweatshirt—right down to panties and an unfortunately accurate AA-cup bra. I gathered up the clothes and folded them. I was slightly embarrassed, but I was also hopeful. Was the plan finally moving ahead?

I said, "Dessi? Are we going somewhere? Are we going outside?"

"We might be."

"That would make sense, wouldn't it? My father is bringing the currency somewhere, to some outdoor location. He's leaving the currency, and you're leaving me. Doesn't that make sense?"

"Maybe. I don't really know." He dumped out the contents of the second WorldMart bag: a large men's sweatshirt with a hood and side pockets. I recognized the colors right away—the University of Miami's orange and green. He muttered, "Looks like I got something, too."

I had to keep him talking. "Yeah? Do you like the U of Miami? I hear they have a good football team."

He answered, "I hear they have a good medical school."

"Yes. That's right. Is that where you wanted to go?"

"I wanted to go there, yeah. I had the grades to go there, too. That was the plan." He paused and added flatly, "Now *this* is the plan."

I cast about for some way to connect to him right then, as a person, as a good person. I tried, "I wanted to be a doctor, too, like my father. But then he turned out to be such a jerk."

Dessi pulled the sweatshirt over his tall, thin frame. "Really? Mine did not. He was far from a jerk. He was a great man."

"What did he do?"

Dessi cocked one eye at me, but then he answered, "He was a teacher, at the Lycée Française in New York. I got to go to school there, too."

"What did he teach?"

"Biology."

"Oh." I knew that the answer to my next question had to be bad, but I asked it anyway: "So what happened to him?"

"He got robbed and killed one night, outside the school, by an ex-student."

"Oh! I'm so sorry."

Dessi shrugged.

"So your life changed then?"

He sat back on the bench, frowning. "Yeah. You could say that. My mother had no profession, no real marketable skills. We wound up moving down here to her brother's house."

"That's terrible."

"No. That's not even the terrible part."

He stopped talking, so I prodded him. "What is the terrible part?"

"She went out to get a job, at a hotel or something. They sent her for a physical. It turned out that the sore throat she had, even when we were up in New York, was not just a sore throat."

He turned around, as if looking through the side of the ambulance. Then he continued. "Her brother tried to get her onto his health-care plan, tried very hard. He even forged a document claiming that she was his wife, but he got caught. He lost his health insurance, too. So she had to go to clinic doctors. Then she died. End of story."

My eyes were tearing up. "That is a sad, sad story, Dessi. How can you tell it so . . . coldly?"

"I have no problem talking about my former life. That person, that person it all happened to, is gone. I have a new identity now. A new life."

I couldn't believe that. "Come on. As a kidnapper?"

He answered sharply, "As whatever I want to be."

"You once wanted to be a doctor—for your father, for your mother. And now you want to be a common criminal?"

He looked me in the eye. "That's right."

"You don't care, one way or the other, what people think of you?"

"No."

"Okay, then. What about God? Do you care what God thinks of you?"

"I don't believe in God."

"Come on! I don't believe that. Not for a minute."

He replied like he was quoting from a book: "There is only the material world and the struggle for possessions within it. The commodities."

I shook my head in disbelief. Dessi just stared back at

me. I finally asked, "What are you talking about? What are commodities?"

"You don't know that word?"

"No."

"Then *écoutez:* Anything that is useful, or that gives one person an advantage over another, is a commodity. Anything that makes one person hand over large amounts of currency to another is a commodity."

"You mean, like me?"

"Correct. Kidnapped rich kids are a definite commodity. That's because people in my world need currency. People in your world don't. They need other things—like rich, dark tans or sparkling white teeth." He added, "Your father deals in such commodities. Does he not?"

"He does," I admitted. "He invented DermaBronze. That's the main reason I'm here."

"There you are." He ticked the next two items off on his fingers. "Education is a commodity. It was available to me up north; it is not available to me down here. Medical care is a commodity. If your little toe gets cut off, you get it sewn up, sterilized; replaced, even. If my little toe gets cut off, I bleed to death. Or some quack clinic doctor sews it up, and I die later of an infection."

I asked him the big question: "So to you, am I only a commodity? Or am I still a person?"

"A commodity."

"And if you have to kill me, you will?"

He looked shocked. "No!"

"But someone will?"

"It will never come to that point."

I didn't believe that. I was getting scared. "Or someone will mutilate me? Let's say my father is too slow delivering the currency tonight. As a warning, someone will cut off my ear and send it to him?"

"No!"

"Or someone . . . Wait! The hell with 'someone'!" I snapped. "We're talking about Dr. Reyes, your so-called doctor. Dr. Reyes will cut off my ear, or he'll cut off the body part that holds my GTD?"

Dessi held up both hands, trying to calm me down. "I don't know anything about any of that. I only know my own part."

"Then let me fill you in. My friend's brother was taken three years ago, and he had his ear cut off. Then he had it replaced with someone else's ear. It's not a pretty sight."

Dessi didn't say anything for a long while. Then he commented matter-of-factly, "Body parts are a big commodity. You can make a lot of currency by selling a body part. I've seen people around here with all kinds of parts missing. I've even heard about kidnappers who do it. It's ingenious, really. They get paid twice. The parents pay them to return the kid, in whatever condition. Then they contact the parents and offer to sell them a replacement body part for the same kid. It's a win-win scenario."

After an even longer pause, I asked him calmly, "Was Albert a commodity?"

"No."

"He had no monetary value?"

"Correct."

"So you killed him."

"I did not."

"Of course not. Dr. Reyes did."

Dessi's eyes rolled upward. He declared, "This discussion is over."

"That's what happened, isn't it?"

"You and I are not discussing anything that will upset you further and perhaps drive you to do something foolish. We are in the endgame now. Understand? It's like the end of a chess game. You and I and everybody else need to play by the rules so it can end . . . the way we all want it to end."

"Do you think this is how Albert wanted it to end?"

Dessi tried to meet my gaze, but he quickly turned away.

"Albert was a great chess player! He was a great mechanic! He was great at . . . putting bandages on kids who got hurt. He was a valuable human being. Do you understand that?" Dessi tried to swat my words away with his hand. "He was more valuable than you, I can tell you that."

Dessi turned completely away from me and pressed his head against the metal wall. I added, more to myself than to him, "He was more valuable than me, too."

I pressed my thumb and forefinger over my eyes and thought, That is absolutely true. What good am I? I'm just a rich kid with bad security. I'm just someone to be taken; someone to be exchanged for a bag of currency.

I thought for another minute about Albert. I thought about my own life ending in an instant, like Albert's. I felt myself sliding down into self-pity, and fear, and paralysis. I couldn't let that happen! I banged my fists down on the stretcher. I took three deep breaths. I shook out my arms and stretched my neck.

Then I forced my mind back to Christmas Eve.

***

Once we had struggled through the ten gross courses of an Edwardian Christmas dinner, Mickie announced, "Attention, everyone! We have a special treat. We will now have after-dinner fun, just as they did in King Edward's time. My producer, Lena, has researched some authentic nineteenth-century parlor games." Mickie held up a stack of cards and fanned them out as Kurt maneuvered for a close-up.

Patience whispered, "I did research on this, too. King Edward was this big fat slob who tried to have sex with all his friends' wives. These games should be pretty good."

I whispered back, "That's a hor-ish thing to say."

"I know."

We giggled as Mickie flipped through her cards and then announced, "The first game is called Blowing the Feather."

Patience and I lost it immediately, turning red and laughing.

Mickie waited a moment, then continued. "Here's what we do. We sit in a circle and try to keep a small feather in the air by blowing at it from different directions."

Patience and I waved our hands and moaned aloud, "No! No!"

"Whoever lets the feather fall gets a forfeit."

Patience made herself stop laughing long enough to tell Mickie, "Sorry, but no. No blowing. No. Not ever."

We giggled even harder, but Mickie did listen to our plea. She put that card in the back of the pile. "Okay. How about this next one. It is called The Courtiers. One of us is the king, or queen, and the rest of us are the courtiers. The courtiers must do everything—and 'everything' is underlined—that the king or queen does. Like yawning, sneezing, scratching, et cetera. Anyone who does not, or"—she stopped to look at us— "anyone who giggles during the game, receives the forfeit."

My father, who I thought was too drunk to speak, interrupted her. "What's the forfeit?"

"It's the penalty for losing."

"Why does somebody have to lose?"

"Because it's a game."

He persisted, "Why does there have to be a penalty in a game?"

Mickie looked into Kurt's roving camera and smiled. "Because that's what makes it fun. Now, who wants to be the first king or queen? Hopewell? Patience? Charity?" We all reverted to our best Mrs. Veck avoidance maneuvers. "No? Mr. or Mrs. Patterson?"

Mrs. Patterson spoke for both of them: "We don't play a lot of games."

Mickie didn't even ask my father. She plunged on. "All right. Just to show you how it works, I will be the first queen. Now you have to copy whatever I do." Mickie sat back and raised up the fingers of both hands until they were even with her cheeks. Then she fluttered them as one unit, as if she were fanning herself.

None of us moved.

"Come on, you courtiers."

For some reason, Patience raised her hands and fluttered her fingers, so I did, too. We burst into laughter as we wiggled our fingers around goofily.

My father then raised his hands up, but he turned his

fingers toward Mickie and fluttered them, as if waving good-bye. He turned to the Pattersons and mumbled, "Resistance is futile, you know. The only way out is death."

Mr. and Mrs. Patterson looked at each other again. Then they reluctantly raised their hands and did a weak imitation of wriggling their fingers.

Hopewell remained slouched forward in his Mrs. Veck avoidance pose, steadfastly refusing to move a muscle.

Mickie continued her fluttering, looking at each of us in turn with a huge, phony smile. "Now let me check my courtiers. It looks like they've all got it except one. Hopewell, honey, I'm afraid you get the forfeit." Mickie lowered her hands, so we did, too. "Okay, everybody? That's how it works."

She selected another card. "Now, the next game is called Squeak, Piggy, Squeak! In this game, a blindfolded person walks around the table, places a cushion on someone's lap, and sits down on it, saying 'Squeak, piggy, squeak!' "

Patience and I had heard enough. We shouted in unison, "No! No!"

The Pattersons looked pretty alarmed, too.

Mickie returned the card to the pile. "Okay. The people have spoken on that one."

Patience whispered, "Can you imagine sitting on Sterling Johnston's lap?" and I doubled over in laughter, gasping for air.

By the time I straightened up, the Pattersons were on their feet. Mrs. Patterson told Mickie, "That was fun, but we really must be going. We have a long trip ahead of us tomorrow. We're driving to Atlanta."

Mr. Patterson added, "We're going to let Hopewell drive

part of the way. We want to make sure he gets enough sleep tonight."

Mickie waved the cards at Mrs. Patterson. "Wait a minute. You can't leave until you pay the forfeits."

I guess Mrs. Patterson had forgotten, or she hadn't been listening, because she asked, "What are the forfeits?"

"The penalties! The losers must pay the penalties."

"Who were the losers?"

"Well, we only played one game, thanks to some giggling girls, and Hopewell lost that one." Mickie flipped through the pile until she found the forfeit cards. "So Hopewell gets to perform one of these."

My father spoke up again. "That might not be a good idea."

"Oh, it'll be fun. And authentic. You were never allowed to leave a party in Edwardian times until you paid your forfeit."

The Pattersons sat down again, grudgingly.

Mickie winked at Patience and me. "Now here's one for the giggly girls. Lena found some naughty forfeits. Naughty for 1900, anyway. Are you ready, girls?"

Patience and I linked arms, pulled each other close, and nodded solemnly.

"The first one is called 'to kiss a lady in rabbit fashion.' For this you need a cotton ball." At the word "ball," we both sputtered. "The lady takes one end of the ball in her mouth, and the gentleman takes the other. They then both nibble toward the middle until they kiss." She stopped and looked at us, surprised. "You're not giggling, girls?"

Patience answered, "No. That's gross."

I added, "And germy. Very germy."

Mickie shrugged. "Okay. How about this one: 'to kiss every lady in Spanish fashion'? The man thinks he's getting off easy with this forfeit, but he has a surprise coming. A volunteer lady leads him around the table to each of the other ladies. But then the volunteer lady bends and does the kissing herself. After each kiss, she wipes her mouth with her handkerchief and then wipes the man's mouth with that."

Patience muttered, "Isn't that 'to kiss a lady in lesbian fashion'?"

Mickie turned our way. Her smile was wavering. So was her tone. "What was that, Patience?"

I froze, but Patience didn't. She looked Mickie, our parlor-game bully, in the eye and answered, "I said, 'Have a gay Edwardian Christmas.'"

I knew Mickie was mad, but she wouldn't show it. She shuffled her deck of cards methodically. "Okay, then. There's one here called 'to kiss a lady through the back of a chair,' but I think we should skip it because it's not appropriate for our group." Mickie produced a card from the bottom of the deck. "Here. Here's the one! We saved the best for last. Get up and join me by the fireplace, Hopewell. This is your real forfeit."

Mr. and Mrs. Patterson stood up, but Hopewell did not. Mr. Patterson finally said, "Come on, son. It's getting late. Get over there and do your forfeit so we can go."

Mickie announced, "While Hopewell is working his way over here, I want to thank you all for helping me test out these parlor games. They're fun, aren't they?" She didn't wait for a reply. "This one is called 'Choose a card.' The person with the forfeit, in this case Hopewell, must stand facing the fireplace while I hold up three cards behind him. One says 'a kiss,' one says 'a pinch,' and one says 'a box on the ear.'"

Mickie showed us the cards to establish that that was indeed what they said. "Now, Hopewell, you have to reach one hand behind you and pick a card. If you pick 'a kiss,' you get a kiss." She turned to me, causing my throat to tighten. "Get ready, Charity."

"Why?"

"Because you're the only young girl who is not a relative. So it will be up to you to do whatever Hopewell picks."

I didn't move. And I wasn't going to move.

Mickie told Hopewell, "Come on, now, reach back." She took his hand in hers and guided it backward toward the three cards. His fingers opened and he picked one. Mickie held it up for us all to see. "Oh no! Unfortunately, you picked 'a box on the ear.'" She playfully slapped his hand. "That's the worst one! What's the matter with you?"

She turned back to me. "Okay, Charity. You have to come and give him a little tap."

"No! Never!"

My father spoke up. "Stop it, Mickie! You've gone too far, even for you. Stop it!"

Mickie stared at us all, clearly not understanding.

Everyone looked away uncomfortably until Mrs. Patterson muttered, "Hopewell had to have an operation on his ear, to repair some damage." Then she added one word: "Kidnappers."

Mickie whispered, "Oh! I'm so sorry. I didn't know that."

The Pattersons gathered themselves together and walked to the door.

Mickie asked Mrs. Patterson, "So what happened to Hopewell? He was . . . he was taken?"

"Yes. I thought everybody knew that."

"I'm sorry. No. All I can think is that my ex-husband didn't tell me. But please, you tell me now. What happened?"

My father assured the Pattersons, "You don't have to tell her anything. This isn't vidcontent we're talking about here, it's your real life. Tell her no."

Mrs. Patterson was red and flustered, but she replied, "I don't mind sharing this. It's important. Everyone needs to know what can happen, what *does* happen."

Mickie continued as if there had been no interruption: "Did you pay a ransom?"

Mr. Patterson answered, "Yes, of course. Immediately."

But Mrs. Patterson contradicted him. "It wasn't immediately. He tried to bargain with them."

Mr. Patterson turned red. "That's not fair. I went right to the vault. I took out all the currency we had."

Mrs. Patterson shook her head adamantly. She told Mickie in a soft voice, "If it ever happens to you, God forbid, just do what they say. Do exactly what they say. Immediately."

Mr. Patterson opened the door and stomped out onto the flagstones. The rest of the Pattersons followed him, silently and sorrowfully. I walked with Patience as far as the gate. She turned and hugged me goodbye. Then Hopewell stepped up to me. He leaned forward, awkwardly, and did the same. I was surprised, but not grossed out. It was a sweet thing to do.

Daphne and Herbert came around from a side door and joined us. They helped the Pattersons climb into the sleigh. Then they trooped off behind the Pattersons, stepping carefully in the slush, as the sleigh jingled away into the night.

When I got back inside, Lena and Kurt were setting up to vid the next phase of the celebration—the Christmas readings. Mickie instructed them: "We'll all gather in front of the fireplace. I'll read some classic passages and then we'll discuss them. We'll edit the content later."

Lena pointed my father to a seat by the fireplace. He was definitely drunk by then but, surprisingly, he did cooperate. He flopped into the leather chair, and I sat on an ottoman next to him.

Mickie stood on the other side of the mantel, in front of Kurt, and held up a book. She began: "Our first Christmas reading is the Robert Louis Stevenson poem 'Christmas at Sea.'" She cleared her throat lightly and read some lines from the poem that I didn't understand at all. She then stopped and looked at me. "Charity, what do you think of that poem?"

All I could think of to say was, "Didn't he write *Dr. Jekyll and Mr. Hyde*?"

"Yes."

"I think I would like that better."

"What?"

"Dr. Jekyll and Mr. Hyde."

"What about the poem?"

"I didn't understand it."

Mickie moved on. She laid the book down and picked up another. "Okay. The second reading is from Leo Tolstoy's *Shoemaker Martin*." She looked sideways at me and added, "In a scene where he realizes that he has met Jesus." She held the book high and read a scene where a guy realizes that all the people he had met that day were really Jesus in disguise. At the end, she turned back to me. "So, Charity, who do you think he met?"

I sputtered, "What?"

"Who visited Shoemaker Martin that day?"

I looked into Kurt's lens and just shook my head. "Are you kidding? It was Jesus! You just told me that."

"It sounds like he had met Jesus several times, but he didn't recognize him. Why was that?"

I threw my hands up.

My father stretched and stood. I thought he was leaving the room, but he was only replenishing his drink from the wine decanter. He pointed his glass at Mickie. "You know, Tolstoy turned his back on his success. He walked away from it all."

"He did?"

"According to what I read."

"What you read? Where?"

"Richter." He explained to me, "The U of Miami library. It had the definitive biography of Tolstoy."

Mickie switched books again. She muttered, "When do you do all your reading? When it's raining on the golf course?"

"No. That one was required in college. I was quite a reader in college."

"Oh? I didn't know that."

He sat back down, slurring his words. "There are a lotta things that you don't know."

Mickie faced the camera again. She held up a small green book. "Finally we turn to the father of the Christmas story, Mr. Charles Dickens. This scene describes Ebenezer Scrooge's encounter with the second spirit, the ghostly spectre." She lowered her voice dramatically and read:

> "From the foldings of its robe, it brought two children; wretched, abject, frightful, hideous, miserable. They knelt down at its feet, and clung upon the outside of its garment.
>
> "'Oh, Man! Look here. Look, look, down here!' exclaimed the Ghost.
>
> "They were a boy and girl. Yellow, meagre, ragged, scowling, wolfish; but prostrate, too, in their humility . . .
>
> "'Spirit! are they yours?' Scrooge could say no more.
>
> "'They are Man's,' said the Spirit."

Mickie closed the book. "What do you think the spectre is talking about there, Charity?"

I was ready for her. "I think you should ask my father. He knows a lot more about this sort of thing."

Mickie smiled tightly. "Fine." She turned to him. "Would you care to comment?"

Dad sat up in his chair and spoke, as if thinking aloud. "Let's see. Mr. Charles Dickens. As I recall, he was a troubled man. He walked compulsively, sometimes all night long, for miles, very rapidly. Near the end of his life he developed a bad foot, so he had to limp compulsively for miles, very rapidly. He never stopped until he died."

Mickie tossed the book down. "Thank you. That was enlightening."

"Wait. I'm not finished." He twirled one hand next to his temple, like a swami. "I'm remembering a college course from long ago." Mickie signaled for Kurt to stop shooting, but my father kept talking. "Ebenezer Scrooge changed because his eyes were suddenly opened by the spirits. He saw the obvious. He saw that we are all fellow passengers to the grave."

Mickie told Lena, "I think we have enough for a show. Let's wrap it."

Lena and Kurt packed up their equipment with practiced efficiency. They were standing at the half-opened front door within a minute, getting the next day's instructions from Mickie. Mickie then returned to the living room and said to me quickly, "Okay. Do you want to open presents now, honey?"

I shrugged.

"Let's open them now. I have to leave very early tomorrow."

"Okay."

Mickie pulled my embroidered stocking down from its hook on the mantel and handed it to me. There was a card inside. I opened it, and a gift certificate fell out. Mickie explained, "It's for Harrods in London—for their satstore, anyway. They have some great things there."

I mumbled, "Thanks."

My father pointed at the mantel. "Look in my stocking.

I hid your present there in case you were snooping under the tree."

I obediently reached inside the *Hank* stocking and pulled up a soft, floppy gift wrapped loosely with blue paper. "What's this?"

He shrugged comically. "Open it and see."

I pulled off the paper and unrolled an article of clothing. A strange one. It was a set of gray thermal pajamas with a black-and-white golf ball on the chest and, at the ends of the legs, a pair of thermal feet. I couldn't help myself. I blurted out, "Feet! What am I, two years old?"

My father shook his head. He assured me, "No. No. Kids your age are wearing these now, especially up north. They're definitely in style."

Mickie interrupted, sneering. "Where on earth did you find those?"

"Myrtle Beach."

Mickie fingered the material with disdain. "They're what? Golfing pajamas?"

"No. They just have a golf ball on the front. Everything in Myrtle Beach has a golf ball on it."

Mickie concluded, "It's a donation-bag item. I'd put it straight in the Kid-to-Kid Day bag."

But I wasn't as dismissive. I did get very cold at night, and I might give the pajamas a try, provided that I could be absolutely sure no one would ever see me in them. I delivered a polite "thank you," and my father returned a "you're welcome."

He then reached over, picked up my Harrods gift certificate, and read the amount. He looked at me, but he was really talking to Mickie. "I hope this comes from the right account. From your ex-stepmother's money, not mine."

Mickie snarled, "How dare you suggest that!"

Albert entered to clean up. Normally my parents stop talking as soon as that happens, but my father continued. "We have a clear division of assets. It is also clear, to those who know how to see, that you are not respecting that division."

"I've heard enough of this."

"The funds are supposed to be frozen, like our marriage."

"If you make any more irresponsible statements in front of witnesses, I'll sue you."

"I don't think so."

Mickie stomped over to the mantel. She pulled two envelopes out of her *Mickie* stocking. She turned and handed them both to Albert with the brief explanation, "Here's one for you and one for Victoria. Merry Christmas."

Albert made a slight bow. "Thank you, Ms. Meyers. Merry Christmas to you."

Mickie then walked straight out of the room, calling over her shoulder to me, "Good night, Charity."

By that point, I was so disgusted that I didn't answer. And she didn't notice.

My father drained another glass of wine and stood staring at the fire. He muttered to me, "You only get one chance to choose your path in life, Charity. I want you to think about that."

I had nothing to say to him, either. Not out loud, anyway. Inside my head I was saying, *You are pathetic. Both of you. What do you want me to do, feel sorry for you?*

For the first time in a long time, I thought about my mother. What had she ever seen in this selfish, shallow man? And what would she think of this woman, this video performer, who he had chosen as her replacement?

Not much, I was sure.

Dr. M. Reyes

Time in the ambulance passed incredibly slowly. I watched the blue numerals fade from 17:10 to 17:11 to 17:12. Dessi was seated with his back to me and his head against the metal wall. I couldn't tell if he was staring at the two-way, doing his sentry duty, or sleeping.

I wondered again: Did I dare to try an escape? Could I slide off the stretcher, moving very slowly? (I thought of a Mrs. Veck moment as she described the killer in "The Tell-Tale Heart" moving more slowly than the minute hand of a watch.) Could I do that until I eased open the door, jumped down, and ran for it? Maybe. Maybe I could.

But I was still wearing footed pajamas.

And I had been trained to cooperate fully with the kidnappers.

And I was, at heart, a sniveling coward.

I soon abandoned any such thoughts and turned my mind to a safer place, Christmas Day at The Highlands.

On Christmas morning, I stayed in bed until 09:00, wishing that both my father and Mickie would leave without feeling compelled to say goodbye. When I got downstairs, my Christmas wish had come true. Mickie was off to her Orlando parade, and my father was off somewhere, too.

Victoria asked me if I had slept well. Then she asked me what I wanted for my Christmas breakfast. I slid onto a stool at the kitchen counter and answered, "I don't care, as long as it's not Edwardian. Something twenty-first century, please."

A few minutes later, Albert served me a cranberry muffin, scrambled eggs, and grapefruit juice. After I finished eating and washed my own dishes, I invited both Victoria and Albert to join me in the living room. They resisted the idea at first, especially Albert, but they ultimately gave in.

Victoria and Albert perched themselves on the edges of two living room chairs like they were ready to run at the first sound of a door opening. I sat on the floor next to our beautifully decorated three-meter Norway spruce, breathing in its sweet scent. Only I knew that there was a present hidden beneath the tree, stashed in a place where no one would ever look.

After some polite chatter with them, I crawled under the shiny boughs and pulled that present out. It was wrapped poorly in some plain green paper, the only wrapping I could find at the time. I handed it to Albert, saying, "It seems that there is still one Christmas present to give out."

Albert frowned. He told me, "Miss Charity, you know

I can't accept any gift directly from you. It's against RDS regulations."

"I know. But this is not from me. So it's okay."

Albert took the gift in hand as I explained: "It's from that girl in Mangrove. The one with the cleft palate. She made me promise to give it to you."

Albert's eyes shifted toward the door, like a trapped animal's. But with some coaxing from Victoria, he finally settled down and unwrapped the gift. After a puzzled glance, he held it up for us to see. It was a wooden *tornada,* with a large *L* carved on the front.

Victoria said, "I remember that girl. She was very pretty. Who was she, Albert?"

"I couldn't tell you. Just some girl. I didn't know her."

"She knew you." Victoria winked at me. "Or maybe she just wanted to."

Albert smiled tightly. "Well, a lot of those kids sure wanted to know you. They always do." He held up the doll again. "So now I've got a fan, too." He stood and made a hasty exit, sliding the *tornada* into his suit coat pocket.

Victoria and I sat in silence for a few seconds. I waited for the right moment to bring up a sore subject. "Victoria? Can I ask you something?"

"Yes, Miss Charity."

"Patience told me . . . that Daphne told her . . . that your father just died."

Victoria's mouth tightened. "She should not have talked about my personal business. That's against regulations."

"Still, I'm glad she did. I want to say that I am so sorry, Victoria."

"Thank you."

"I would like to hear a little bit about your father."

"I'm afraid that would—"

"Be against regulations, too?"

"Yes."

We sat in silence again while I worked out a plan. "Okay, then. Listen: I have a paper coming up for Mrs. Veck."

Victoria looked at me suspiciously. "Oh yes? What is it about?"

"It's about the global community. We each had to spin the globe and put our finger down on a random spot and write about someone from that spot. I have to write about a man living in Mexico City. Can you tell me a little about a man living there so I can use it in my paper?"

Victoria knew I was trying to con her. "Miss . . ."

"Because I don't have any idea what his life would be like. For example, what would he do for a job?"

She sighed. "A job?" She glanced at the door and then at me. "A job. All right. A man there might sell something."

"Yes? Sell what?"

Victoria smiled sadly. "He might sell *naranjas*." She translated for me: "Oranges."

"And how would he do that?"

I had her hooked now. In a soft voice, she explained, "He might walk to the market and purchase one hundred *naranjas;* he might carry them to a street corner in a wealthy area; he might sit by the curb and sell them. If he sold two hundred pesos' worth, he made his money back. If he sold more, he made a profit."

"Would he have a shop, or a stall, or anything?"

"No. Just a curb on the roadside. To every car that passed, he would call out, *'¿Quiere usted una naranja?'*"

I nodded. "Excellent. That's excellent information. And what would the man's wife do?"

"She would be at home. With their children."

"How many children?"

"Maybe two."

"A boy and a girl?"

"Maybe two girls."

"Would they be really poor?"

"No. They would have a good home. Each girl would have a dress for church and a school uniform. Their mother would walk them to school every day."

I started to ask another question, but she interrupted me. "And that's all you will get from me for your paper. Now go write it for Mrs. Veck."

"Thanks, Victoria."

"Yes. Thank you, too."

I was still smiling, remembering that exchange, when Dessi broke into my thoughts. He was tapping on the foot of the stretcher. When I looked up at him, he said, "You need a bathroom break."

I answered, "I need a bathroom. I need a few minutes of privacy. I need to brush my teeth, damn it."

"Sorry. You know how it has to be."

"Come on! *You* go to a bathroom. There must be one right outside!"

He just repeated, "Sorry."

"Then forget it. I can wait."

"You're supposed to be drinking your SmartWater. Three bottles a day, for complete nutrition."

"Well, I'm not."

"I know you're not. You don't want to get dehydrated. The doctor would not like that."

That word really offended me. "The doctor? How can you call that criminal out there 'the doctor'?"

Dessi shrugged.

"Doesn't that bother you?"

"No. It's just a word, like any other word."

"Excuse me, but no. It's a title. A title that should be earned."

Dessi's lip curl returned. "Spoken like a true Highlands girl. You've never gone to a clinic doctor. Have you?"

I admitted, "No."

"If you had, you'd know it's just a word."

"Oh yeah? A word, let's say, like 'kidnapper'?"

Dessi's eyes twitched slightly.

"You don't like it when I call you that word, do you?"

He answered defiantly, "I would rather you called me that word than some others."

"Like what?"

"Like 'servant.'"

"Really? You think 'servant' is something shameful to be?"

"Yes. And so do you, if you're being honest."

"Absolutely not!"

With a dismissive wave of his hand, Dessi pulled down the bench and sat. I figured he was through talking, but I was wrong. He pointed an accusing finger at me. "Would *you* be a servant?"

"Yes."

"An RDS servant, with the fake costume and the fake name and all?"

"Absolutely. I work with Victoria all the time. I'd be just like her. I'd work at RDS and save enough to go to college."

"Really? You would come down from your throne and work for a master?"

"I would work for *myself*. At an honest job. And make my own currency. There's absolutely nothing wrong with that."

"Oh no! Things have gotten so much better for the servant class. I hear some of them even get health care." Dessi held his hands up. His palms were very white. "Did you know that the servants of an Egyptian pharaoh, when the pharaoh died, had to march into his pyramid with him, get sealed in there, and then slowly die of starvation so that they could continue to serve him in the land of the dead?"

"No."

"Nowadays, when servants die, they get to stay dead. They don't have to serve anymore. So yes, I suppose *that* part of the job has improved."

I shook my head at his hypocrisy. "You're the one who looks down on servants. Not me."

"That is such *mierda*. Such *merde*. You look down on anyone who isn't from your economic class. Everyone except Ramiro Fortunato. He's admirable to you. Why? Because he defends all the rules that keep you on top."

I repeated his words from earlier: "How could I admire him? He's not even a real person."

Dessi leaned forward, engaging me. "Okay. That's true. So tell me, who is a real person who we can all admire?"

I shrugged.

"Who is the most admired person who ever lived?"

I reverted to my Mrs. Veck form, looking away and muttering, "I don't know."

"Yes, you do. It's Jesus."

"Okay."

"Jesus was born a poor boy, and he died an even poorer man. The Roman guards took away his last possession, the clothes off his back. He had absolutely nothing left. *Rien*. That's what makes him such a great role model, right?"

I shrugged again.

"He was the son of God, and yet he was content to be poor as dirt. That's a powerful message to send to a servant, isn't it? 'What are you complaining about, poor boy? Jesus himself was poorer than you, and he is the most admired man who ever lived!'"

"That's not why people follow Jesus."

"Maybe not. But it's why people like *you* want people like *me* to follow Jesus."

"Jesus never kidnapped anybody. I can tell you that."

Dessi ignored my comment and continued, "Now, who is the most admired American who ever lived?" This time he didn't wait for a reply. "Abraham Lincoln. Every year, in every poll, he wins the prize. Why? Because he was the poor boy who made it. He was born with nothing, but he educated himself, and he grew up to be the President of the United States!"

"That's a good thing, right?"

"Wrong."

"What about the President we have now? He was poor. And he was black."

"He still is black."

"Yes. So that means the poor can still make it. So what's your point?"

"That you will use this one poor boy as a role model for us all. However, the dirty little secret, the thing that you will not tell us, is this: You're only going to let one poor boy succeed. The other fifty million poor boys who work like slaves to overcome poverty and racism will fail. They will not become the President. And they will blame themselves, never realizing that the deck was stacked against them all along."

"So what?"

"So what!"

"Yeah. So maybe they don't become President of the United States. I'm not going to be President, either. But they can become something else, something productive. They sure don't have to become kidnappers."

This time his whole face showed the sting of my words.

I went on. "They don't have to waste their lives sitting around feeling sorry for themselves, like some people."

He snarled at me, "Like who?"

"Like you. You feel so sorry for yourself because you're not in college. So why don't you get into college? You had some hard times, sure. Some really bad things have happened to you. But you could work to overcome those things, like . . . like Ramiro Fortunato."

"Don't talk to me about that fool!"

"Then like Abraham Lincoln. No. Instead, you turn to kidnapping, and robbery, and murder."

"I am not a murderer!"

It was my turn to snarl at him. "And then you sit here, Mr. I Know Everything About Everything, and try to defend yourself! Blaming everything on your top four layers of derma."

"My what?"

"Your skin color. That's all it is, four layers of derma, with active melanin molecules."

Dessi actually looked at the skin on his arms and then back at me. "You don't know what you're talking about. Racism is about a lot more than skin color."

"And your poverty. Let me tell you something. You don't look that poor to me. You sure don't sound it. I don't know any kid who has the education you do. You know biology, and history, and politics; you speak French. You have no excuse for staying poor."

"Oh no? How about that somebody shot my father dead? How about that somebody let my mother die because she had no currency?"

I waited a suitable time to say, "I'm sorry. Those were really bad things."

"Tell me about it, little rich white princess."

"But my mother died, too. Long before yours. And my father—well, my father is lost to me in a very real way. He's only around to pay the bills."

Dessi sat back in his seat. *"C'est vrai."* He pointed over at the clock. "That's what he's around for, all right. To pay the bills with a big bag of currency. That's what we're here for. And the sooner we can make that happen, the better."

I agreed. *"C'est vrai."*

Dessi flipped open a book—the only book around, my Ramiro Fortunato novel—and started to read. I assumed that our conversation was over.

I looked at the vidscreen. The red light was on. The blue numerals now read 17:30. *Oh my God,* I thought. *Is that all it is?* I felt tears welling up in my eyes. How much longer did I have to wait? Six more hours? I pressed the palms of both hands against my ears until the thrumming of the ambulance engine was replaced by the sound of my own rushing blood. And I concentrated harder than ever on the past.

As planned, I spent all of Christmas week at The Highlands with Victoria and Albert. Patience was in Atlanta, so despite Victoria's daily prodding, I made no effort at all to get out and live my life. I had no adventures. On the positive side, though, I had no night terrors.

I did get to help Victoria with a big domestic project. She and I spent three days "canning preserves," a nineteenth-century activity right out of *The Manor House Four-Season Cookbook.* We sliced up apricots, pears, and mangoes; boiled them in a pan with white sugar and pectin; then poured the contents into color-coded glass jars. It was hard, sticky work, but it was fun. Especially when Albert passed through the kitchen and we both fell under his disapproving gaze.

Mickie and my father were both gone for the first part of the week. Mickie traveled to Orlando and then to New York to rehearse for that Times Square broadcast. She burst through the door on December thirtieth, announcing to no one in particular that she had to "rest up for a day! Do nothing for a day!"

I guess that's what she did. I didn't see much of her. But because she was at home, I had to stop helping Victoria in the kitchen.

I don't even know where my father was for the first part of the week. I know he flew his helicopter to West Palm Beach to play golf on the twenty-ninth. He didn't return until late afternoon on the thirty-first. I think he had been drinking. He handed a suitcase full of dirty laundry to Albert and went upstairs to sleep. He got up and packed to leave again a few hours later.

The only thing he said to me was in the foyer, at the door. He turned and asked, "Have you tried out those thermal pj's yet?"

"No," I admitted.

"It's supposed to be cold tonight." He stood for a moment and waited for me to commit to wearing them, so I mumbled, "Okay. I'll put them on tonight."

He smiled. "You'll be glad you did." Then he raised his eyebrows ridiculously high and shouted, "Go, Canes! National champs!" I smiled weakly, and he headed out the door.

Confident that no one but Victoria and Albert could possibly see me, I went upstairs and dutifully pulled on the gray pajamas. I stood before my full-length bedroom mirror. The feet looked hideous, like a storybook monster's, and the golf ball called attention to my flat chest, but I definitely felt warm and comfortable in them.

I padded downstairs to the kitchen for an early supper. Victoria and Albert both smiled at my choice of clothing, but the only comment was from Victoria: "I'll bet those feel real comfortable."

"They really do," I conceded.

Victoria and I sat together at the kitchen counter and ate roast beef sandwiches with potato salad. Albert sat at the small kitchen table and ate the same. For dessert, Albert poured us all cups of eggnog—regular for Victoria and himself and a special chocolate one for me. We agreed to meet in the living room later to watch the Mickie Meyers special from Times Square.

But that was never to be.

On my way upstairs after supper, my stomach started to gurgle and churn. It felt like it was twisting itself into a knot. A few minutes later, I was sitting on the toilet in my bathroom with the grossest case of diarrhea in medical history. Victoria brought me two anti-diarrheal tablets to try to stop the mass evacuation of solids and fluids from my body, but the tablets didn't do any good.

At 18:30 Albert touched a thermometer to my ear. He told Victoria, "It's one hundred point five."

Victoria put her cool hand on my neck. "Should I call Mr. and Ms. Meyers?"

Albert shook his head. "Ms. Meyers is in the middle of two hundred thousand people. Mr. Meyers is at a big party, too."

Victoria insisted, "Still, that's the protocol. We have to try."

Albert exited and returned quickly with a securephone. Victoria typed in my father's number, followed by Mickie's number. Then we waited. After about three minutes, Victoria broke the silence. "Okay, Miss Charity, we'll keep trying. For now, you need sleep more than anything else. We'll be back to check on you."

As soon as they left the room, I fell deeply asleep.

I do remember the two of them coming back in the dark. I sat up groggily; my mouth tasted totally disgusting. Victoria held a glass of water to my lips and gave me two more anti-diarrheals.

Albert took my temperature. Then he whispered, "One

hundred and one. A half point higher. Let's check it in an hour. If it goes up, we'll call the parents again."

I must have passed out after that, because the next thing I knew they were back in my room and I could hear gunshots from outside. Some of our Highlands neighbors greeted each new year by firing Glocks into the air. It must have been exactly midnight.

This time, I felt Victoria's small hand touch the thermometer to my ear. She emitted a gasp. Albert immediately whispered, "What?" He stared over her shoulder at the thermometer's readout. Then he made a decision: "All right. We have to take action. You try to reach the parents. I'll call the hospital."

Victoria corrected him. "No, that's not the protocol. If I can't reach the parents this time, we have to follow the protocol, to the letter." She punched the same two numbers into the securephone, but she didn't wait nearly as long to decide. "They're not answering. All right. You need to call the hospital from the securephone, and you need to patch the guardhouse into the call."

Albert agreed: "Right."

"Tell the hospital to send an ambulance right away."

I watched Albert's long fingers punching buttons on the phone. He spoke into the receiver in his most formal voice. "This is the residence of Dr. Henry Meyers in The Highlands. This is a simultaneous call to the Martin County Regional Hospital and the Highlands security office. Do you both acknowledge?" After a brief pause, he went on: "The security code for this emergency is one-one-two, three-five-eight. Do you acknowledge?"

Then he told the hospital operator, "I need an ambulance at this residence for a thirteen-year-old female. She is experiencing diarrhea and a high fever, one hundred and two point five Fahrenheit. She has ingested four fifty-milligram tablets of an anti-diarrheal, the latest dosage shortly before zero hundred hours."

Victoria interrupted him. "She has the flu. Tell them she has the flu."

Albert frowned, then added, "We believe she has the flu. Yes. Yes, I understand. All right." I heard a beep as Albert hung up. He told Victoria, "You have to be careful how you word things with them."

Victoria applied a wet washcloth to my forehead. It felt cool and very good. "Why? What do you mean?"

"We said the word 'flu' to them. That makes this an infectious-disease call. They have to wear hazard suits."

"Fine. They can wear whatever they want just as long as they get here fast."

"I just don't want Miss Charity to be alarmed by the sight of them. That's all. They'll look like men in space suits."

Victoria moved the cloth down to my neck. She whispered, "You're going to be okay soon, Miss. The doctor is on the way."

"Two doctors," Albert added. "That's their protocol for The Highlands. If they can't spare two doctors, they send a doctor and a nurse."

"Two is better still." She leaned over me and explained, "This is some messy flu bug you have. They'll find out which one, and they'll give you the right treatment for it."

Albert said, "I'll pack her bag."

Victoria instructed him, "Put in her vidscreen, in case

she's there overnight. And her toothbrush and toothpaste. And a book." She turned back to me. "Albert will be with you the whole time. Don't worry. He'll ride right there in the ambulance. I'll get your father and Ms. Meyers on the phone soon. Everything's going to be all right."

I tried to nod, but my head felt very heavy. I was in a total mental fog. I have no recollection of the Highlands guards arriving, but they suddenly were there in my room in their black shirts, pants, and boots.

Then two men in green hospital scrubs entered, pushing a stretcher. One was short and stocky; the other was taller and thinner. They wore surgical face masks and caps. I watched groggily as the guards inspected the men's Martin County Regional Hospital badges. A guard read each one aloud: DR. M. REYES for the shorter man; DR. LANYON for the taller one.

The two ambulance men took positions on either side of my bed. They pulled out my bedsheet and rolled it toward me until I had a tube of white sheeting running up each side of my body. Then they emitted a collective grunt and slid me horizontally onto the waiting stretcher.

Dr. Reyes bent over me. He lifted my eyelids and felt for a pulse behind my ear. He swabbed my arm with an alcohol pad. I felt a prick as he quickly slid a needle into my vein and taped it in place.

Dr. Lanyon hung a plastic bag of clear liquid over me, on a metal rod. After some fumbling, he connected a tube from that bag to the needle in my vein.

Victoria spoke to Dr. Reyes in Spanish: something like, "¿Cómo está ella?"

But it was Dr. Lanyon who answered, in a light Indian-accented voice: "This will keep her hydrated on the ride. Blood-testing at the hospital will determine her course of treatment. Who is the family physician?"

Victoria answered, "That would be her father, Dr. Henry Meyers."

"All right. We will contact him on the way."

"You may not be able to. Not for a while."

The two men never said another word. With Victoria, Albert, and the guards preceding them, they wheeled me out of the room.

Looking back on this scene, I can say that I felt something was not quite right. Even in my fogged state, I had some doubts. Why were Dr. Lanyon's hands trembling when he hung up my intravenous bag? Why didn't Dr. Reyes speak? And, more significantly, why did Dr. Reyes, the last one out, place an envelope on my unmade bed?

I remember rolling through the marble foyer and past the stained glass of the front door. I remember the diesel engine of the ambulance running. I remember the black smoke blowing across my face. The ambulance had the words MARTIN COUNTY REGIONAL HOSPITAL painted across the side, in orange letters with black highlights. The two doctors lifted me up, slid me inside, and locked the wheels of the stretcher in place. Then Dr. Reyes closed the door without saying a word, leaving me back there alone.

I could hear the guards asking the doctors to sign some forms, and I could hear Victoria speaking impatiently to Albert, something like, "What's taking them so long? This is an emergency!" I heard her say, "I'm going inside to call the parents again. Take care of her, Albert."

Finally, the Highlands guards left.

I remember that the doctors and Albert all climbed into the front cab.

I remember that we stopped at the guardhouse, and I heard Albert speak briefly to someone there. His voice sounded strange. Was he worried? Nervous?

I heard the gates swing open as we drove out.

Somewhere just beyond the gate, I fell deeply asleep. Obviously, there must have been a powerful sedative in that plastic bag. I remember nothing else. But it probably doesn't matter. According to my kidnapping training, it was all over at that point, that point just beyond The Highlands' gate. The kidnappers had succeeded. I was in their hands. I was their prisoner.

I had been taken.

Saint Elmo's Fire

At exactly 18:00 Dessi stood up, snapped his two-way closed, and pointed at my pile of WorldMart clothes. "They just said that you need to put on the new clothes. Right now. So I need to give you some privacy."

That was fine with me. I was about to mutter "Okay," but he slipped out before I could even open my mouth.

I listened to be sure the ambulance door clicked closed.

I checked the vidscreen to be sure the red light was out.

Then I set to work quickly. I peeled off the top of the golf pajamas and, with my hands shaking, hooked on the bra and pulled the T-shirt over my head. Then I slipped out of the footed bottoms. I pulled on the panties, jeans, and sneakers in just a few swift moves. Even while keeping an eye on the back door and the vidscreen, I managed to complete the entire transformation in less than one minute.

I stood with my back to the red light and looked down at myself. The simple act of putting on clothes, even these WorldMart clothes, made me feel much better. I kicked the footed pj's under the stretcher. I ran my hands through my grungy hair, finger-combing it as best I could. I took my index finger and scraped at my teeth, too, for whatever that was worth. I had just finished when Dessi returned. He sat back sullenly in his chair. I waited for him to look at me, or to say something, but he did not.

After about one minute of waiting, I gave up and climbed onto the stretcher again. As soon as I did, though, the red light *did* blink on. It watched me for about fifteen seconds and went off.

Then, without warning, things got very weird and very frightening.

Dessi jumped up and stood as if at attention. His eyes darted to a spot directly behind me. He stared at that spot dumbly, like he was getting a set of instructions that he could not understand.

Coming from that same direction, from the ambulance cab, a figure entered my field of vision. It was the stooped figure of Dr. Reyes, dressed as always in his hospital scrubs.

I watched in rising fear as he opened a cabinet door and pulled out a contraption that he quickly assembled into a standing metal table. He placed the table next to my head. He placed a package on top of it, a sterile-wrapped package with rows of sharp objects visible inside. Then he reached under the stretcher and snapped a latch that made it fall back flat. I fell back with it, too frightened to do anything at all. I felt him reattach the leather strap around my waist.

Dr. Reyes studied my face briefly through a dark plastic visor, but he didn't say a word. He turned and opened the other cabinet and removed two items—a coil of clear tubing and a plastic mask, the kind they use to give anesthesia.

Dessi remained standing there, straight as a pole, just staring at us both.

It wasn't until Dr. Reyes pulled on a pair of surgical gloves that I truly realized what was happening. My worst fear of all. *Oh my God,* I thought. *This is it. He's going to cut into me! He's going after my GTD.*

The last thing I remember was him connecting the tubing to the wall outlet, placing the mask over my face, and holding it there. After that, I was nowhere. I entered a state of delirium. Crazy images flashed through my brain, and then one not-so-crazy image: I had a revelation.

I saw myself back in my bedroom at the very start of my ordeal. I was watching Dr. Lanyon struggling to hang the IV bag over me. His green scrubs slid down along his upraised arm, and I saw his dark, dark skin. I recognized that skin, those four layers of derma.

Dessi.

Dr. Lanyon was Dessi. I told myself, in my delirium, *You have to remember this.*

I drifted in and out of consciousness. I felt a pair of hands working on me, like a mechanic working on a car, swiftly and efficiently.

Eventually, I woke up enough to focus on the vidscreen. It

showed 20:55. I had been out for nearly three hours. My mind felt surprisingly clear, though, like the anesthesia had already worked its way out of my system. I even felt momentarily elated.

Then I remembered where I was, and what had just happened to me. Dr. Reyes. The surgical knife. The search for my GTD. It all came back to me like a wave of nausea. Had I been mutilated? Where? What part of my body was missing?

I started to wiggle my toes frantically. Were all ten there? It felt like it. My fingers? Yes, all ten. What about my earlobes? I turned my head and scraped it each way against the sheet. Yes, they were both there, and intact. I ran my tongue over my teeth, poking around them for several seconds until it hit me: My braces! My braces were gone.

As if he could hear my thoughts, Dessi spoke up from his seat. "That's right. It was in your braces."

I lifted my head up, very carefully. "Huh?"

"The GTD. It was in your braces." I didn't answer. I laid my head back down heavily, and he continued. "I had braces, too. Back when we had the currency for such things."

I rolled my head back and forth slowly, trying to gather my thoughts. I finally asked him, "What did it look like?"

"What? The GTD?"

"Yeah."

"It looked like a little piece of metal, like a ball bearing."

"Was it in a tooth? Like a filling?" I felt around with my tongue.

"No. It was hidden inside the wire that held your braces on. That was a smart move. Placing a GTD within a metal wire actually increases its broadcast range."

I was starting to feel better, well enough to try to sit up.

Dessi saw my efforts and came around to help. He undid the leather strap around my waist; then he latched the back of the stretcher at an angle so that I could pull myself to a sitting position.

I asked, "So what happens to it now?"

"To the ball bearing?"

"Yeah."

"It goes away. Far away." Dessi backed toward the door. "I'm supposed to report in as soon as you're awake."

"Why? To who?"

He seemed to consider giving me a real answer, but then he just muttered, "You'll see."

"Who? Who do you have to report to? Reyes? What's going on?"

"Relax. There's just something that you need to know."

He left me alone for about five minutes. I enjoyed the feeling of sitting up straight. I actually thought myself lucky to lose my GTD so painlessly. Luckier than Hopewell, anyway.

Then the back door opened.

I peered into the dark. A shape filled the doorway. It was not Dessi's shape, and it was not Dr. Reyes's. It was a taller, broader figure; a big man. He pulled the door shut behind him and turned around, and I screamed. I screamed like I had seen a creature risen from the grave.

Because it was Albert.

All I could do was babble, "Albert?"

He stared at me blankly, like a zombie.

"I thought you were dead," I told him.

After a long pause, he spoke in a voice as deep as my Albert's, but different. "Albert is dead, yes. But *I'm* not dead."

"What?"

"I was never really Albert. I think you know that."

"Well, yes, I know it was just your work name. Oh, Albert, I am so happy to see you alive!" I wanted to run to him. To hug him. But he looked away. "What did they do to you?"

"Who?"

"The kidnappers. Did they lock you up somewhere?"

Albert stepped closer so that he loomed over me. "You need to know what's going on here."

"I'm so glad to see you safe."

"You need to know that *I* am the kidnapper."

His words did not register at all. "What?"

"*I* am the kidnapper."

I stared at him for a long moment. Then I finally understood. "No!"

"Yes."

"No!" My eyes started to fill up with tears. "No, you can't be!"

His voice hardened. He answered like he was giving instructions to a lawn guy: "We don't have much time. You need to know the facts: I am *not* dead. I am *not* Albert. I *am* the kidnapper. Understand?"

I was frightened by his voice. I answered meekly, "Okay. Yes."

"Your father has agreed to our terms. He has agreed to pay us a ransom, after which you will be released unharmed. Understand?"

"Yes."

"Your parents have been given a packet of very specific instructions telling them what things to do, and in what order."

"Yes? Was that in the envelope?"

This seemed to throw him off balance. "What?"

"The envelope that Dr. Reyes left on my bed?"

"You saw that?"

"I did."

His eyes shifted to the door and back. "Yes, well, you're right. That envelope had instructions for the payoff. It names the location for the payoff, and it describes a backup plan if necessary. The payment is to be made by your father, alone, from his helicopter. He will fly over a secluded area. He will lower the currency down on a wire. When we have the currency, you will be released."

Albert extended his big hands outward. "That's it. That's everything you need to know. For now, you need to rest. You've been through a lot." He spoke with such authority that I automatically closed my eyes. I soon fell back to sleep.

I awoke at 21:21. Albert was still with me, seated on Dessi's pull-down bench. He addressed me right away in his no-nonsense voice: "Charity? Do you remember the conversation we had earlier?"

It sounded odd to hear him call me by name, without the "Miss." I answered, "Yes."

"So you understand who I really am?"

"Yes."

"And you understand what we are going to do next? The payoff plan?"

I nodded, but I didn't say anything. I couldn't. My eyes were welling up with tears again. After about two minutes of staring at him, I finally choked out, "Do you have any idea what you put me through? I cried my eyes out for you! I cried

148

at the thought of your dead body lying in a ditch by the side of the road."

Albert looked down. "I am sorry you did that. But now you know it didn't really happen. It was merely a feint, like in a chess match." He leaned forward in his seat and stole a look at the clock. I guess we had some time to kill, because he asked me, in a kinder voice, "So, do you have questions? You must have questions."

Of course I did. But this was too bizarre for words. This man was Albert! He had lived with me for the past three years. He had served me my meals. He had protected me with his life. Suddenly, in an instant, he had become a totally different person. He had become his own opposite. I didn't want to talk to him at all. But I needed answers, so I finally replied, "My GTD. Obviously, this 'doctor' didn't cut into me. I still have all of my body parts. How did he know where it was?"

"Your father told us."

"Really? I'm surprised he remembered."

"Your father has been totally cooperative in every way. Now that we're in touch with him, things should go smoothly."

"Wasn't he at his big football party?"

"Yes. But we were able to reach him. He has canceled all other activities until he gets you back."

I felt brave enough to ask him what was really on my mind. "And what if he didn't answer your call? Were you just going to kill me?"

Albert's whole demeanor changed. He replied indignantly, "No! Never. We knew he would call back. We knew everything would go just as it has."

"How? How could you be sure?"

He took a breath to calm down. He answered quietly, logically: "Because I know your father. You are his daughter, his only child. He would do anything to get you back. And because I know your family. Things are very predictable in your family at this time of year. Dr. Meyers is at the Orange Bowl Fest; Ms. Meyers is in Times Square; you are at home, alone with the help."

I didn't like that. "'The help'? You're talking about yourself, I hope. Not Victoria."

"She's the help, too."

"You're not telling me that Victoria had anything to do with this!"

He emitted a short, unhappy laugh. "No. No. Victoria is true blue, all the way."

"Yeah. Like all RDS employees swear to be."

"That's right. She bought into the deal one hundred percent."

"But you didn't?"

"I did for a while. But then things changed."

"Why?"

"Let's leave it at that."

"You became a kidnapper instead."

"I said, let's leave it."

"Okay. How many of you are there?"

"How many of me?"

"Kidnappers."

"Oh. I can't tell you that."

I raised up my fingers as I counted. "There's you, Dessi, Dr. Reyes, Monnonk, a guy on guard duty up front. Anyone else?"

He stood up. "That's enough questions for now."

"I have one more."

He answered reluctantly: "Okay."

"Do you really think you'll get away with this?"

"Yes. Like I said, it's perfect timing. Your parents are working through a messy divorce. There's still a lot of currency to be divided up. The assets are liquid and accessible. So we will take some and disappear."

"They'll catch you. Eventually."

"Who?"

"The security forces. The police. The FBI."

"Is that what you learned in your training?"

"Yes."

"Then learn this: The security forces, the police, and the FBI will not come after me unless your father or your ex-stepmother tells them to. Your father and your ex-stepmother want nothing to do with the FBI or with any branch of the government. I know for a fact that they are both cheating about the currency. They're both dipping into frozen funds. Neither one wants the Currency Authority looking into this. Believe me."

We both turned at the sound of a gruff voice outside. Albert lowered his voice. "Listen to me. You don't want to cross paths with that doctor. Okay? Got that?"

"Okay."

"You do all your communicating through me. Don't even look at him if you don't have to. Don't let him think you could ever recognize him again. That would be very dangerous."

"Okay." Then, as Albert grabbed the door handle, I said, "Albert?"

"What?"

"I can't keep calling you that name. What else can I call you?"

"Don't call me anything."

"But I might have to. Just give me a temporary name."

"Temporary?"

"Yes. For today only, because I'll never see you again after this. It can be another made-up name, you know, like your butler name."

"I don't think that is necessary."

"Or it could be the name of some hero of yours. Or even of a chess piece that you like. Just something. Anything."

He laughed that unhappy laugh again. "All right: Mantlè. You can call me that."

"Mantlè?"

"Right. It's Creole."

I knew damn well it was Creole, and I knew what it meant. Albert had given himself a hortatory name: Liar.

Albert opened the ambulance door and slipped out. A minute later, I heard the driver's-side door of the cab open; then the passenger side. Through the metal, I could hear Albert's low voice, mixed with Dr. Reyes's loud grunts. Then I heard the buttons of a securephone being pushed. They were making a call together. It only took me a few seconds to guess who must be on the other end.

My father.

Dr. Reyes growled at him to "follow the orders exactly."

I couldn't understand my father's reply, but I could hear his voice. Faintly. And I could hear the fear in it.

I heard Albert tell him, "Check the weather alerts. Go

over the flight plan in your head. No. No! You are not to file a flight plan. The instructions say that clearly. Officially, this flight is not happening. Understand?"

My father's voice quavered as he answered, "Yes."

"The drop spot is at the bass lake, on the south side. I'll have the GTD with me. Watch for its signal so you'll know where to drop the currency. Understand?"

"Yes."

"Be there at midnight. At twenty-four hundred hours. Not five minutes after; not one minute after. If you are late, the results could be tragic. Understand?"

And, one final time, I heard the frightened voice: "Yes."

I knew that voice—distracted, half listening, like he always was with me. I prayed that he would concentrate on the instructions and follow them exactly.

Then I lay back again, to wait.

I found myself thinking about Patience: *She's the most impatient person I know. She could never wait like this. She'd go crazy.*

I thought about the third syllogism in our game. It's called the Hypothetical Syllogism, and it's the most complicated one. It requires two *If . . . then* statements, like this: "*If* my father does not concentrate, *then* he will not deliver the currency. *If* he does not deliver the currency, *then* I will get killed."

To complete the syllogism, you combine the first and second, like this: "*If* my father does not concentrate, *then* I will get killed."

At exactly 23:00, Albert opened the ambulance door. He stuck his thumb up. "All right. It's all set." He climbed back inside, closed the door, and sat on the bench. "Your father has his instructions; your ex-stepmother has hers."

153

"Mickie? What is she doing?"

"Ms. Meyers is at your house in The Highlands. She will watch the transaction on a securescreen. We will watch her watching the transaction on our own vidscreen."

"Will Victoria be there?"

Albert hesitated for just a second. "Yes, I suppose so."

"Will she be able to see me?"

"They will be able to see you."

"So am I supposed to beg or plead or something?"

"No. That won't be necessary. Everyone will be exactly where he or she is supposed to be; everyone will do exactly what he or she is supposed to do; and everything will go fine."

He looked away. I wondered if he really believed all of that. He looked back and spoke to me kindly: "Listen. You're a good girl, a good person. You always have been. This is just business. You understand?"

"Yes."

"And we are going to take care of business in about one hour."

"Okay. Just tell me what to do, and I'll do it."

Albert nodded. He placed his pointer finger on the vidscreen clock: "Here's the timeline: Your father has filed a flight plan from Miami to The Highlands for tonight. He will arrive at your house in The Highlands at twenty-three forty. He will walk around to the front door and ring the bell. He will pick up a trash bag filled with currency from Ms. Meyers. Then he will take off in his helicopter again and use his GTD tracker to locate me. I will be waiting at the assigned spot, holding the GTD itself."

Anticipating my next question, he told me, "You will be

waiting at a second spot with Dessi and Dr. Reyes. Your father will lower the trash bag on the wire rope of the helicopter. I will inspect its contents; then he will take off.

"Ten minutes later, you will be released unharmed with your vidscreen made fully operational. You may then use it to contact your father or your house or any police authority. They will come and get you, and your ordeal will be over."

"Good. Let's hope it all happens like that."

He asked me pointedly, "Why wouldn't it?"

I didn't like his tone, so I sat quietly for a minute.

He broke the silence by saying, "By the way, there is some news from The Highlands, news that you should hear. Your classmate Whitney Rice was taken from a vacation resort in the Berry Islands. The family paid the ransom and she was returned, in one piece, within twenty-four hours. That's what's going to happen with you, too. Okay?"

"Okay."

"This is the endgame now." Albert got up and opened the back door. He looked left and right. He made a low whistling sound.

I heard footsteps, and then Dessi appeared in the frame of the doorway. "What is it, Monnonk?"

"I need you to sit with her."

"Sure." Dessi climbed in and resumed his position on the bench. He didn't look my way.

I finally said to him, "Monnonk? That's Albert's real name?"

Dessi continued to avoid my eyes. "No. It's Creole. It's a shortened form of the French *mon oncle*, 'my uncle.' "

"Okay. What does he call you?"

"Neve. It means 'nephew.' "

I thought about that, and I had another revelation.

How could I have been so stupid?

I asked him, "So if he's Monnonk . . . how many kidnappers are there, exactly?"

"Three," he admitted.

I was flabbergasted. "What? Three? How can that be? Who . . . who is sitting in the front cab?"

"Nobody."

"Who is sitting at the other end of the two-way?"

"Nobody."

My mind went spinning back through my ordeal, from the beginning. "You! You were Dr. Lanyon. I figured that out."

"That's right." Dessi re-created his bit of dialogue for me in pseudo-Indian: "This will keep her hydrated on the ride."

"But the—"

"I can't answer any more questions. I shouldn't have answered those."

"Why? Because everything's on a need-to-know basis?"

"Exactly."

"Why?"

"So that the plan can proceed smoothly; so that no one gets hurt by doing anything foolish. We're all in this together now."

"No. I'm not in this with you! You forced this on me, and my family, and everyone who knows me."

Dessi stood up. "This is not a good use of our time. You can't afford to get upset right now. I think we need to just sit quietly. Or we could play chess. I have a set nearby."

"No."

"No, you don't play?"

"I'm not playing a game with you! Are you out of your mind?"

156

Dessi held up his white palms. "Fine. We can watch some vidscreen." Without waiting for my consent, he leaned over and pulled up the Justice Channel.

I just sat there, reeling from the latest revelation and from the shock of my own stupidity.

I stared at the screen absently. The Justice Channel was broadcasting something called *Speakers' Corner*. We watched a man sitting on a wooden chair against a gray stone wall. He started reading from a legal pad in a low, quavering voice. He apologized to his family and to the families of his victims.

After a few minutes of that, Albert opened the door. He stood there for about fifteen seconds. Then he asked, "What are you watching?"

Dessi answered, *"Speakers' Corner."*

"What is that?"

"It's a reality show, for prisoners."

"Prisoners?"

"Yeah. They get to make a final speech before they get the needle."

Albert looked appalled. "Do you really think that's appropriate to watch now?"

Dessi answered seriously, "Yes, I do. I think we should be totally aware of what we're doing, and its consequences."

Albert stared at the screen again. "So who is that guy?"

"A murderer, probably."

"They're going to show him getting executed?"

"No. They're just showing his last speech before he goes into the death chamber. It's like Speakers' Corner in London. That was the last stop before the gallows, where the condemned had a chance to address the crowd."

Albert watched for a few more seconds. Then he decided, "No, this is a bad idea. Shut it off now."

Dessi hesitated, just for a second. Then he shut it off. But he protested: "Come on, Monnonk. We can't just sit in here and stare at each other."

"Why don't you get the chessboard? Charity knows how to play."

"She's not interested."

"Okay, then. You should rest. The both of you. I'll be back in a few minutes."

Albert closed the door. Dessi stood still for a moment with his back to me and his arms extended upward, pushing into the roof of the ambulance, making it bow out. Then he turned around. He was angry at Albert, but he took it out on me. He snarled, "Why do *you* need to rest? All you've been doing is lying there."

I had taken enough crap off him. I snarled back, "Really? All you've been doing is sitting there."

Dessi stood at the foot of the stretcher. His lip curled high. "Okay. I have a few things to say to you, little rich girl, if you're up to it."

"If I'm up to it? Things like what? Like you're sorry for being a kidnapper? And a thief? And a liar?"

"That's what you think, isn't it? That *we* are the criminals?"

"Yeah. That's what you are. What do you think?"

"That *you* are the criminals! That you have broken your word; broken the contract."

"What contract is that? The one where, if you don't get everything you want, you can start killing people?"

"No, like my mother will have a minimum of health care; like I will have a minimum of opportunity."

"You have as much opportunity as I do!"

"You are rich and white. You have unlimited opportunities. I am poor and black. I have to chase after one of the opportunities set aside for the poor and black."

"Oh? Okay. And how do you keep your end of the contract? By getting an education and learning a skill and getting a job? Like my father did? Like my mother did? Or by robbing the people who worked hard to get those things? You're a . . . common thief. A *vòlè*. A lazy common thief!"

Our exchange ended right there because the ambulance door was thrown wide open. Albert climbed in and snapped at Dessi, "I can hear you two yelling from the outside! I thought I told you to rest."

Dessi didn't answer.

Albert looked from him to me. "It's time to stop the nonsense. It's time to get down to business. Let's get this done." He pointed at my vidscreen. "You'll need to have that with you. Everybody will be watching a screen; everybody will be on a camera. There will be no surprises anywhere."

Dessi moved up to the front cab. I supposed he was going to drive, like he had at the beginning of my kidnapping. Albert's eyes followed him. Then we both heard the door to the passenger side slam. Dr. Reyes must have climbed in.

Albert sat on the fold-out bench. He turned the vidscreen toward himself and searched for something, muttering, "I've been checking the weather alerts. There are thunderstorms around, with high winds, so we need to get in position fast."

Suddenly, with a lurch, the ambulance started moving. We drove for about five minutes, with Albert still staring at the screen. He finally said, "You'll be able to watch what is happening at The Highlands." He turned the screen toward me. "Look."

I wasn't prepared for what I saw. There was Victoria! She was sitting in our living room, right where she had sat on Christmas morning. She looked very pale except for the dark circles under her eyes. Mickie was sitting next to her, looking tense and angry.

I watched as the two of them stared into their own vidscreen. My red light was not yet on. Were they just staring at nothing, waiting? Neither moved for several minutes. Then, at exactly 23:40, the doorbell at our house rang.

Albert told me quietly, "This is all part of the instructions. So far, so good."

Victoria stood up. She turned the vidscreen so that its camera could follow her actions. She crossed the marble foyer and opened the tall oak door, revealing a short figure.

It was my father.

He looked pale, terrified. He stood in the doorway, weaving slightly, like he might be drunk. His clothes looked disheveled; sweat was pouring off his face.

Victoria took two steps left, toward the garage, and pulled a black trash bag into camera view. She tipped it so that its contents became visible. I saw a great pile of currency notes—dollars, yuan, rupees, euros—probably the entire contents of our vault.

Victoria then sealed the top of the bag with a steel clamp that I recognized. It was from my father's drone helicopter. It was used to raise and lower things on the wire pulley, the one that could rescue drowning kittens.

My father took one step inside, lifted the bag up, and started back out the door.

Victoria retrieved the vidscreen from the living room and hurried to follow him down the flagstone path. She caught up to him while he was fumbling with the gate latch.

Once through the gate, he turned left, walked the length of the front yard, and then turned left again, following our wrought-iron fence to the helipad where his Robinson Beta Five sat. The camera watched his every step as he lurched off into the night with the bag slung over his shoulder, like a Santa Claus without a suit.

Victoria zoomed in closer, and I watched my father reach the Robinson Beta Five, distinctive with its U of Miami logos. He loaded the bag into the back and struggled to attach it to the wire rope. Then he climbed into the pilot's seat, started the motor, and rose jerkily into the air.

The last scene Victoria filmed was the Robinson speeding away to the southeast, to its rendezvous with us.

At the same moment, our ambulance was speeding down a bumpy road with lots of turns. I dared to say to Albert, "So we're heading toward Deep Lake?"

He looked startled. "How did you know that?"

"I heard you tell my father. On the phone."

"I said 'Deep Lake'?"

"No. You said 'the bass lake,' but I knew where you meant. We stopped there on Kid-to-Kid Day. It's the one with the killer fish, right?"

"Right." He snapped, "What else did you hear?"

I suddenly got scared. "Just my father's voice."

"Nothing else?"

"No. Nothing."

"That's a good answer."

I stole a look back at the screen. Victoria was now back inside and sitting next to the fireplace. She was fingering a white rosary and praying. Mickie was sitting to her left. For the first time in her life, and probably the last, she looked better than Victoria.

We drove along silently for another five minutes; then the ambulance came to a stop. Albert handed the vidscreen to me with a warning. "Pay very close attention to what is happening. And do exactly what we tell you to do."

I nodded. Albert opened the back door, jumped out, and closed it quietly. Immediately after, I heard the cab door open and close, too. Then the ambulance started to roll again, but not for long. I felt us bumping over ruts, like we had gone off-road. Then I felt us backing up.

As we came to a stop, the red light blinked on. Victoria could see me now! And Mickie. What was I supposed to do? Wave? I figured I wasn't supposed to do anything, and I didn't. After a few seconds, the full image of Victoria and Mickie shrank and moved to the right side of the vidscreen, and a new image appeared on the left side. It was a view of an open field taken by a vidcamera placed somewhere behind the ambulance.

Dessi entered from the front cab and sat next to me on the stretcher. He leaned over so that he, too, could see the screen. He said, "If you look at the left side, you can see Albert there, waiting. You'll be able to hear his communications, too."

I followed Dessi's finger and saw Albert's silhouette in the field. Every few seconds, he became illuminated by a flash of distant lightning. The wind was whipping his shirt and pants. He was looking to the north and holding something out in his left hand, perpendicular to his body.

I pointed to his hand. "What is that?"

Dessi squinted. "I don't know. It looks like some wire, maybe. Maybe to secure the bag of currency."

I stared harder at his hand. Then it hit me. "No. That's orthodontic wire."

"What?"

"Those are my braces!"

"They are?"

"Yes. That's kind of disgusting. I thought you said they threw them away."

Dessi sounded embarrassed. "That's what they told me. But I guess not. I guess I didn't need to know that part." A few seconds later, he added, "But it makes sense. You know? That's how they'll zero the helicopter in."

"Right. Albert told my father, 'I'll have the GTD with me.' That's how they're going to do it. My father has the tracker with him. When he's right over the GTD, he'll lower the money."

A brilliant flash of lightning lit the field. It was followed by a thunderclap close by. Then fat raindrops started to fall on the metal roof of the ambulance. At 23:59, the helicopter appeared in the distance. It grew larger on the vidscreen until it was hovering directly over Albert, whipping the rain and wind around him even more.

My father seemed to be having trouble steadying the helicopter. After about thirty seconds, though, a wire rope did appear, dropping down in jerks from above. It had a trash bag attached to it. But then the wind whipped up mightily. The chopper lurched upward and backed away, and the bag jerked upward with it.

I heard Dr. Reyes's voice growling angrily: "What is he doing? Is he drunk?"

The helicopter, trailing the long rope and bag, managed to ease its way back to the clearing. In the distance, a bolt of lightning cracked to the ground.

Albert's wind-whipped voice replied, "He's struggling with the downdraft."

"I can see that! Can he do it?"

"Yes. He just has to adjust. He can do it. Any pilot can."

Dr. Reyes shouted, "This one is a fool! I can't watch this. I'm going back." I could see him leap into view on the vidscreen and start scrambling over the dirt field quickly, like an ape. Then he slipped out of our view as he reached the front cab, opened the door, and climbed in, cursing the weather.

The Robinson hovered above Albert again, and the bag started to lower again. Dessi and I both leaned in to stare at the screen. The wind was howling outside. This time we watched the helicopter jerk to the left, far to the left. It seemed to get caught up in the wind and to be carried away like a toy, all the way to the metal towers.

Suddenly the helicopter's dangling rope began to rise on its own, like it was being drawn by a magnet. Before I could even shout out a futile warning, the rope got too close, and a bolt of electricity arced out from the high-tension wires.

My mouth fell open as I watched the horrible sequence of events that followed: The electricity ran up the wire like a squirrel up a branch. When it reached the top, the whole he-licopter glowed briefly with a pulsing metallic blue. All I could think of was a Mrs. Veck science lesson. I could hear her de-scribe a ship struck by lightning as having "the glow called Saint Elmo's fire."

Two seconds later, the helicopter exploded.

Dessi shouted, "Oh my God!"

He jumped up and started toward the back door.

I jumped off the stretcher, too, ready to follow; ready to do anything to help my father.

But Dr. Reyes shrieked at us from the front, "No! Stay where you are! Both of you!"

Still standing, we turned our faces back toward the stretcher and watched the screen. The red light remained on, recording my look of horror as, in one long and agoniz-ing shot, my father's helicopter flew away like a flaming bird. It started to spiral crazily out of the sky, losing altitude rapidly in a diagonal path. Then it crashed headlong into the center of Deep Lake.

I looked to the right of the screen, at Victoria's face. She was totally stunned. She was making the sign of the cross rapidly and praying in breathless Spanish. Mickie's face was just frozen.

I was too shocked to do anything but keep breathing in and out.

Dessi sat down heavily on his bench. He told me, in a bro-ken voice, "It . . . it was an accident. You saw it. He got too close to the wires. What was he doing? He shouldn't have been anywhere near those wires."

I found my voice quickly. I answered, "What was he

doing? He was doing what you *told* him to do. Because if he didn't, you would kill me!"

"No. No. You saw it. It was an accident. It wasn't supposed to happen."

Dessi fell to his knees and banged his head and shoulder against the door. Hard. "Oh my God! Forgive me. Oh my God."

Dr. Reyes entered from the front cab, moving slowly and heavily, with his back turned toward us. He picked up my vidscreen and stared directly into the red light. Then he delivered a short, somber message to Mickie and Victoria: "Listen to me. Look at your instructions. Plan B is in the envelope. Read Plan B very carefully. We are now following Plan B."

Albert

By 00:10, I was supposed to have been freed by my captors. I was supposed to have been on my way back to The Highlands. And to Victoria. And to my life. Instead, I remained trapped inside a white metal cave, living a nightmare as bad as any night terror I'd ever had.

The sight of my father's death kept coming back to me, rerunning in my head, and it got worse every time. At what point did he die? Did he die in agony, burned, electrocuted? Could he have still been alive when the helicopter crashed? And then did he die in the cold, black water of the lake? It was all too horrible. Too horrible.

I lay on the stretcher and agonized over these questions as we drove out of the field and sped off back to the kidnappers' lair. Once the ambulance stopped, Dr. Reyes, snarling and cursing in Spanish, jumped out immediately. Albert waited a minute, perhaps trying to work up the courage to face me, but he never did. He, too, exited without so much as a glance into the back.

I was left with Dessi, who at least had the decency to be crushed by the night's events. He was still on his knees, half leaning against the door, when his two-way rang, startling him. He managed to open it and croak "Yes?"

I could hear Albert's voice giving him instructions. That bastard. He was talking like nothing had happened. Dessi whispered, "I will, Monnonk," and hung up.

Dessi took a deep breath. He placed his hands flat on the floor and pushed himself to a standing position. He folded down the bench and flopped onto it. Then he turned in my direction and muttered, with his eyes downcast, "You are to drink a bottle of SmartWater and go to sleep. If you need something to help you sleep, Dr. Reyes will give it to you."

I told him, "Go to hell."

"No. No." He shook his head. "Don't cross Dr. Reyes. He will force you to do what he says."

"He can go to hell, too. In fact, I'm sure he will. You all will."

"Please. Please." Dessi's voice dropped to a whisper. "We were never going to hurt you. Or anyone. That was just talk."

"How do you know?" I shouted. "What if you didn't know about that part, either? What if you didn't need to know what your leader, that murdering doctor creep, had planned?"

"I know . . . that I would never have let him hurt you."

"Oh, you wouldn't? Let me tell you something. You don't know crap, Mr. I Speak French, Mr. I'm Too Good to Speak

Creole. You're not too good for anything. You're nothing but a low-life criminal. You'd do whatever you were told."

Dessi shook his head miserably. He finally whispered, "You had better keep your voice down."

"Why? What are you going to do?"

"Nothing. It's Dr. Reyes. He'll do something, believe me."

"You're afraid of him?"

"Yes." He inclined his head toward the outside. "I need to call him and say that you are asleep. Otherwise he's going to come in here and—" He lifted one finger and pointed at the cabinet door and the oxygen gauge. "You don't want that, do you?"

I exhaled angrily. "No."

"Then drink some of that." He pointed to a bottle of SmartWater on the ledge. "And lie down and pretend to sleep so I can call."

"Right. Your drugged water? Sure, I'll drink some of that. I'll drink it all. Anything to get away from you." I unscrewed the bottletop and drank the colorless, tasteless liquid down in two big gulps. I didn't want to lie down, because I knew the images of my father's crash would come back to me, fiercer than ever. But I couldn't bear the thought of that plastic mask being forced down on me, either, so I did lie back.

Dessi flipped open his two-way. Before he spoke, he told me, "You and I have one more thing in common now. We have both lost a father to violence."

"Right," I said. Then I reminded him, "But I had no part in your father's death."

He answered miserably, "Right." Then he called Dr. Reyes and lied for me.

I fell asleep shortly after that, due to the water or to sheer exhaustion. I had no night terrors. Maybe when your real life becomes the terror, there's just nothing left to dream about.

I awoke to a gentle rocking motion and a scratching sound, like a tree branch brushing against metal. I listened to the noise for a long time, waiting for my head to clear. I looked over at Dessi's chair. He was still in it, tilted backward, snoring quietly with his mouth open. Without thinking too much about it, I slid off the stretcher and crept past him. I slowly turned the door handle, eased it open, and slipped outside.

I saw why the ambulance had been rocking. Someone, probably Albert, had painted over the MARTIN COUNTY REGIONAL HOSPITAL design and stenciled the words ALL-NATURAL ORGANIC FERTILIZERS — BELLE GLADE, FLORIDA in their place. Was this part of Plan B?

I stretched out my arms and legs, grateful to be out of the white cube of the ambulance. Judging by the sun, it was about noon on a clear and cold day. My mind was still aching with the thoughts of my father's death. But behind those thoughts, and pushing to the foreground, were new thoughts. Thoughts of survival. Should I just take off and run? But run where? I didn't even know where I was. Should I take a chance that someone, some stranger, might help me? According to my training, that would be risky. I could wind up dead, or taken again, and the cycle would start all over. I couldn't bear that.

No. As bad as it might be, Plan B was still better than no plan. I decided to cast my fate with Plan B. And with Albert.

I looked around. I was on a muddy driveway, between the ambulance and a house. The house was made of concrete blocks painted yellow. It had rust stains all along its bottom edge. An old car was parked in front of the house. It was a German car, I think, although it was so beat-up-looking and dirty that I couldn't really tell.

There were two other houses across the way, set about twenty meters back from the street—one white and one green. They, too, had rust stains down by the grass line. No one seemed to be stirring in them, or anywhere else on the street.

After screwing up my courage, I opened the screen door of the yellow house and walked into the kitchen. Everything looked surprisingly neat, considering that this was the kidnappers' lair. A row of spice jars sat in a rack on the right wall, above a dark brown boiler/freezer. On the left wall were a sink, a water purifier, and a dishwasher. All of it seemed color-coordinated, perhaps with a woman's touch.

I crept across the tile floor until I was standing in the archway to a living room. Unlike the kitchen, this room was a total mess. It was filled with tubes, circuit boards, wires, scanners. I knew enough about doctors' offices to recognize what all the objects had in common—they were parts from medical equipment.

At the far end of the room, in front of its only window, was a sleeping figure in a black recliner.

Albert.

As if he sensed my presence, his eyes snapped open. He looked confused at first; then angry. He hissed, "What are you doing here?" His eyes shot to a hallway entrance along the right wall.

I pointed toward the same spot. "Who's in there? Dr. Reyes?"

Albert leaned forward in the recliner until he was sitting upright. "Yes. He's just gone to sleep. So keep your voice down. Now tell me immediately, what are you doing here?"

I stepped over some wires until I was in the middle of the room. "Dessi is still asleep."

"Asleep!"

"So I came to talk to you."

"That's very dangerous."

"This is all very dangerous. Isn't it?"

Albert looked me in the eyes. Then he got up and cleared some wires from an ottoman. "All right. You can sit here if you like, and we can talk quietly." I sat down on the edge of the ottoman and waited. Albert finally said, "What did you want to talk to me about?"

I looked into his eyes and told him, with barely controlled rage, "What do you *think* I want to talk about, Albert? You killed a man last night. You killed my father."

His hand shot upward and turned on its edge, like he was trying to deflect my words with a sword. "What happened last night was an accident."

"The 'accident' happened because you kidnapped me. You started a chain of events that resulted in my father's death. You don't need to watch the Justice Channel to know the rest, Albert. A death that occurs during a kidnapping is considered a murder. Period. You committed a murder. All three of you.

"The only thing you can hope for now is mercy. And the only way you're going to *get* mercy is to *show* it, to let me go. You could say you did not mean to cause the first death, and you saw the error of your ways, and you refused to cause a second death."

Albert shook the sword-hand at me. "First of all, there's

not going to be any second death. And as to the first one, your father bears some of the responsibility for it."

"No. He does not."

"He does. He does, and that's all we're going to say about it."

I kept staring at him, challenging him, waiting him out until he spoke again. He finally lowered his hand and continued, in a sinking voice, "Charity, I am sorry. If I could let you walk out right now, I would. But that would mean that this was all for nothing, including your father's death. The only way out is Plan B. We'll get another bag of currency; you'll be set free; we'll disappear."

Neither one of us spoke for another minute. I let my eyes wander over the array of machine parts. I finally asked, "Why, Albert? Why did you . . . betray me like this?"

His eyes flickered toward the hallway again. He asked me, "Has Dessi told you anything about his parents?"

"Yes. Some. He said his father was murdered in New York. His mother died down here."

"That's right. Did he tell you that his mother was my half sister?"

"He said she was your sister."

"That's right. We had different fathers, but to us there was no 'half' about it. Our mother died when I was eight. She was eighteen, so she took care of me. Later, when her husband died, she had no place to go. I had this house, so I took her in. Her and Dessi. I knew as soon as I saw her again that she was sick. She called it a sore throat, but there was no way a sore throat would go on for that long."

Albert paused for a moment and looked away, perhaps

thinking of his sister. When he turned back to me, though, his voice was crisp. "Did he tell you what happened next?"

"He told me you tried to get her covered by your RDS health-care plan, but you couldn't."

"Did he tell you I lied to them?"

"Yes."

"That's right. I did. To RDS, and to the doctors, and to the voices on the other end of the health-care lines; to all of them. I lied through my teeth, trying to save her life. So they kicked me out of my plan, and they tagged my file at RDS." He explained, "That meant that my current job would be my last job; they wouldn't reassign me. They also notified my employer." He paused for emphasis. "But nothing came of that. I guess Dr. Meyers had more important things on his mind.

"With no health-care plan, we had to go to clinic doctors. We spent three months making the rounds from one incompetent fool to another." He pointed toward the hallway. "Then I heard about one in Miami named Dr. Reyes. I heard he had an operational DBS. Do you know what that is?"

"No."

"A digital body scanner. Dr. Reyes, using that DBS, was able to diagnose my sister in just one visit. She had lymphoma, cancer of the lymph nodes. That was no surprise to me. I suspected it, but I couldn't prove it.

"She should have had that diagnosis six months earlier, back in New York, back when the doctors could have done something about it. There are treatments that would have kept her alive, possibly cured her altogether. But by then it was too late. She was dead one month later. It wasn't peaceful, and it wasn't pretty.

"Dessi took it very hard. So did I. I wanted to do something about it, and I don't mean a crime or a murder or anything like that. I wanted to do something positive. I wanted to make good come out of bad.

"So I went back to Miami. I started talking to this Dr. Reyes. He had a working DBS. Why didn't other clinic doctors? We came up with an idea. He had access to medical equipment. It was mostly used, broken medical equipment, but it was the real stuff. And it was fixable. All we needed was some technical knowledge and the currency to buy parts. We started talking about where we could find that currency."

He paused significantly, as if he had just explained everything away. I wasn't buying it. I answered, "So you figured you could just kill the family you've lived with for three years, and take their currency to buy your spare parts, and that would be a positive thing?"

"No, of course not! No one was supposed to get killed."

"What about Plan B? Does anyone get killed in that?"

He hesitated for a fraction of a second. "No. No one else is going to die."

I feared that hesitation, but I pressed ahead. I asked the most practical question I could think of: "Where will the second bag of currency come from?"

"From the sale of your house. From what I hear, it's coming from Mr. Patterson's vault."

"I see. So does Patience know about this?"

"She shouldn't. Not if Ms. Meyers follows her orders; not if Mr. Patterson can keep his mouth shut."

"Those are big ifs."

"It doesn't really matter. The payoff will be tonight, at nineteen hundred. You'll be free by nineteen-ten."

"I've heard that before."

"You will be."

"There's no Plan C?"

"No."

"Then you will take your currency, disappear, and enter the health-care field?"

"That's right."

It all sounded too simple to me. After another minute, I asked him, "So what about Dessi? What'll he do?"

"I don't know. That will be up to him. He is very independent." He pointed outside. "Young men and women around here basically have two options—be a servant or be a soldier. One is degrading; the other is deadly."

"Which do you think he'll pick?"

He answered right away: "Soldier."

"Why?"

"Because someone will *ask* him to pick that."

He gestured at the medical parts on the floor and explained, "If you lived in this house and you called a doctor, you'd wait the rest of your life for one to come. Literally. But if you called a military recruiter, he'd be here inside an hour. And he wouldn't be alone. They'd be lined up outside your door—army, navy, marines, air force. They'd make you feel very, very wanted."

He added sadly, "That's a powerful feeling for the young people down here. So maybe Dessi will go that route. Maybe he'll do his bit in the Oil Wars. Ironically, he would get excellent health care. He might lose his life getting it, but . . ."

"But what?"

"But at least he wouldn't be a servant." Albert got up. "All right. That's enough. You need to go back to the ambulance now and stay there." He reached over to take me by the elbow, but I pulled back.

I said, "Wait. I need to use a bathroom. A real bathroom. Will you at least let me do that?"

Albert nodded courteously. "Of course. It's the first door to the left, down that hall. I'll have to stand outside, though."

"Okay. If you have to."

I followed Albert's directions down the dark hallway and turned left. The bathroom was really gross. It smelled like mildew, and it had fungus growing in the tub. There was definitely no woman's touch in there. I finished up quickly and exited.

I walked ahead of Albert through the kitchen and into the daylight. The sun was directly overhead, blazing down on the driveway, evaporating the muddy water. Albert warned me, "Don't even think about running for it."

"I'm not. I could have run for it earlier, but I didn't."

He assured me, "You wouldn't have gotten very far."

I looked him in the eye and told him, as sincerely as I was able, "I believe in you, Albert. I believe in Plan B."

"Good. You won't be sorry. Drink some fluids and sit tight until evening. Then we'll get this done."

Albert watched me open the door and step up. I didn't even try to sneak back in. I didn't care anymore. Albert slammed the door behind me, startling Dessi and waking him. Dessi's hands flitted around his face like he was being attacked by bees. "What? What's going on?"

"Nothing's going on."

"What are you doing? Get back on the stretcher." I climbed up and sat back against the incline. "Are you trying to escape?"

"No."

Dessi stood up, yawned, and stretched. He asked me seriously, "Tell me what's going on. Did I fall asleep?"

"You did."

"What did you do?"

"I had a long talk with Albert."

"Oh no! Where?"

"In the house, the house full of medical equipment."

He nodded fatalistically.

"I know a lot more than I did last night."

Dessi placed both hands behind his back and stretched again, making his vertebrae crack. "I guess he's mad at me now."

"I wouldn't worry about it."

"I would."

"Why?"

"He's my uncle."

"Oh? What does that mean?"

"It means . . . your uncle is like your father. You don't want to disappoint him."

"Albert is like your father?"

Dessi looked at the door. "I don't know. Sometimes I think yes. But sometimes I think . . ."

I felt sorry for him at that moment. I said, "Well, the truth is, he just spoke very highly of you."

"Really?"

"Yeah."

He gulped and nodded. Then he went back to sitting in silence. I started to think about my father again, but I fought off the impulse. Instead, I pulled the Ramiro Fortunato novel from my backpack. For the next three hours, I stared at its simple illustrations and its bilingual text, and I thought about its simple message of heroism.

At 15:05, Albert came in to relieve Dessi. He muttered, "Go take a break, Neve." As Dessi slipped out, Albert took his seat and asked me, "How are you doing?"

"Fine."

"Rested? Ready for tonight?"

"I've been on a stretcher for two days. I'd say I'm rested."

"Good. We all need to be alert and ready tonight. No mistakes."

I curled my lip like Dessi. "Mistakes?"

"I'm sorry. I didn't mean anything by that."

We heard a quick rap on the back of the ambulance. Then the door opened slightly. Dessi whispered to Albert through the crack, "Monnonk, you're not going to believe this."

"What?"

"Look at your vidscreen. I'll turn on mine and vid them."

"Who? Vid who? What's going on?"

"You had better look for yourself."

Albert leaned across the stretcher and worked the vidscreen. I saw a view of the street come up, and then I saw something unusual: a second car was parked outside, a car that had not been there before.

I looked closely at the screen. I recognized that car! But I didn't let on to Albert. It was a Ford 900D, the work car for the number one realtor in Martin County, Mr. Roy Patterson. What was he doing here? Was he selling a house in Mangrove?

Dessi remained just outside the ambulance door, vidding the scene. He widened the view, and I saw a figure standing by the front door of the white house. The figure had an unruly clump of brown hair and singularly bad posture. The figure started to back away from the door, moving in a familiar, invertebrate sort of way.

It was Hopewell! I couldn't control a gasp at the sight of him.

Albert looked at me, and then at the screen. "Who is that? Do you know?"

I mumbled, "I might."

"Is it a boy or girl?"

"I think it's a boy."

He leaned closer to the screen. "Hopewell? It can't be. Is it Hopewell?"

"I think so."

"What's he doing here?"

"I have no idea."

We watched Hopewell backing up steadily. Then we saw why he was in retreat. Two boys and a girl had come out of the house. One boy in the lead was pointing a menacing finger at Hopewell, and he seemed to be yelling at him. The sight of the boy jogged my memory, and I quickly realized why: he had been doing the exact same thing on Kid-to-Kid Day when the mob turned on Hopewell and Sterling Johnston.

This time, however, the scene unfolded differently. After a few more steps, Hopewell stopped backing up. He stood rigidly still, with the boy still yelling in his face. When the boy finally stopped, Hopewell lifted up his left hand and showed some papers to the group.

Albert muttered, "What the hell is that? What's going on?" He stuck his head out the door and whispered, "Neve! Zoom in on those papers."

Seconds later, the camera snapped into focus on a set of flyers. Although blurry from the motion of Hopewell's hand, it was obvious who they were about: me. Hopewell was showing "Taken" flyers of me—with my face; with my height, weight, and hair color; with everything that goes on a "Taken" flyer.

I wanted to cry.

Albert knew what the papers were, too, and he wasn't pleased. He told Dessi, "Okay. Enough. Zoom out."

The camera pulled back, and we were soon looking at a changed scene. There were now three boys and two girls around Hopewell. They were listening to him, but just barely. He was clearly not a welcome visitor.

Suddenly the first boy flashed a backhand at Hopewell that sent the flyers scattering along the ground. Hopewell bent to retrieve them, trying awkwardly to gather the papers in his arms. Some had fallen on a tall boy's foot. When Hopewell reached toward them, the boy kicked the flyers away and then kicked Hopewell in the backside.

Others in the group started to laugh nastily and to encircle him. But then we saw another surprise. A girl came charging into the frame—just over one and a half meters tall, curly blond hair. It was Patience, my best friend. She threw a vicious punch at the boy who had kicked Hopewell. Then one of the girls jumped on Patience's back.

Albert opened the door and whispered orders to Dessi. "Neve! Give me the vidscreen. You go across the street, double-time! Stop this thing before it gets any worse."

Dessi protested, "What can I do?"

"Tell them to leave those kids alone! You're bigger than them. Threaten them if you have to."

"Can't you come with me?"

"I can't. Those white kids are from The Highlands. They know me. So it has to be you, and it has to be now!"

Albert took the vidscreen in hand. He leaned out just far enough to keep vidding. I watched Dessi run across the street, shouting and waving his arms. Patience was now wrestling on the ground with the girl who had jumped on her back. Hopewell had gathered up all the scattered flyers. He wasn't fighting, but he wasn't running away, either.

The group turned as one to watch Dessi's approach. He continued to shout and to gesture at them. The girl let Patience up and pushed her roughly toward Hopewell. Dessi herded Patience and Hopewell back toward the street, placing himself between them and their attackers. The worst seemed to be over.

Then Hopewell handed a "Taken" flyer to Dessi. I watched Dessi look at the picture and read the words. I watched him shake his head no and hand it back. The big liar. *Mantlè!* Dessi pointed at the Ford 900D with both hands and talked animatedly until Patience and Hopewell got back into it. Albert turned the vidscreen slightly so we could follow as the big car drove away. I watched until it was completely out of sight.

Dessi returned quickly, panting. "I did it, Monnonk. The white kids left."

"They left?" Albert asked. "Or they went to the next block?"

"I don't know. I tried to scare them. I told them to get out of here; that they didn't belong here; that they'd get hurt here."

"Good. Good. Those were all the right things to say." Dessi climbed inside. Albert shot an angry look at me. "What the devil were those kids thinking of?"

I told him, "Saving their friend's life."

"Hopewell Patterson. Of all people!"

"That's right. Hopewell and Patience Patterson. They're prime targets for kidnappers, aren't they?"

"That's right. They are."

"But they stood up anyway, didn't they? They stood up for what's right. Like Ramiro Fortunato."

Albert tried to wave my words away. "I just hope they got some sense scared into them out there. Hopewell's been through it before. He should know better."

"He should know better?" I spat out. "Is that what you're saying? He should know that you should trust your kidnappers? Trust them not to hurt you?"

Albert's jaw muscles tightened. Then, without another word, he snapped the vidscreen shut and hurried out of the ambulance. Dessi seemed puzzled by my sudden anger and by his uncle's retreat, but he didn't say anything.

After a few minutes, I had calmed down enough to ask him, as matter-of-factly as I could, "So, tell me something: how did I look on my flyer?"

He shrugged. "Not too bad. You looked a little younger. And you had braces."

"Uh-huh. What did Hopewell say to you?"

"Something like, 'Have you seen this girl? She's been taken.' "

183

"Right. And what did you say?"

"I said no."

"Mantlè."

"Come on. What else could I say?"

"Did Patience say anything?"

"No."

I stared hard at him. I knew enough about his face by now to accuse him. "You're lying again."

His eyes flashed angrily. "You don't need to know everything that she said."

"Yes, I do. She's my best friend. Tell me."

After a long pause, he muttered, "You won't tell Monnonk?"

"No."

"She didn't say anything to me. But she said something to him."

"To Hopewell?"

"Yeah."

"What?"

"She said, 'Come on. We've got more flyers to pass out.' "

I started to choke up. I managed to say, "That's, uh, that's really brave."

Dessi pulled down his seat. "I think that's really stupid."

I didn't answer him. I reached around the stretcher and undid the latch. Then I lay down, face first, to hide my flowing tears.

Victoria

At 18:45, Dessi and Albert were both standing outside, on the driveway. I could see them through the rectangular frame of the open ambulance door as they whispered to each other intensely, like the Dugans with an evil secret.

Albert looked up at me. Nervously? Suspiciously? I couldn't tell. All he said was, "It's time to get ready, Charity. Come on, I'll walk you over to the bathroom."

I pointed to my backpack and answered, as reasonably as I could, "Please. This is beyond disgusting. I haven't brushed my teeth in two days."

Albert thought for a moment. "You're right. Sorry. Your toothbrush and toothpaste are in there. Bring them along." Dessi looked down at the ground as I grabbed my nearly empty backpack and climbed out of the ambulance. I didn't like the look on Dessi's face. Or Albert's. What had they been talking about?

Outside, it was already dark. A bright half moon was rising in the east in a clear sky. The other two houses on the street already had dim yellow lights burning inside.

Albert walked me back through the house, stepping over wire and plastic to the gross bathroom. I stayed in there for about five minutes. I brushed my teeth and mouth very thoroughly and went to the bathroom, running the water the whole time so Albert couldn't hear me. When I finished, I opened the door and had a sudden shock.

I was staring into the dark face of Dr. Reyes, or what I could see of it behind his surgical mask and glasses. He looked from me to Albert and back. He was definitely not pleased that I was in the house, away from my ambulance prison, but he didn't say anything.

When Albert and I got back outside, Dessi was already in the driver's seat of the repainted ambulance/fertilizer truck. Albert opened the back door for me to climb in; then he followed. We took our places and waited in silence for two minutes until we heard Dr. Reyes climb into the front cab. Then Dessi backed the truck out onto the street and drove us away.

Albert continued to stare at the floor, which made me feel very creepy. What was he really thinking? What happened to the optimism of 'You'll be free by nineteen-ten'? What happened to 'You won't be sorry' and 'We'll get this done'? Were those just more lies? Lies upon lies? I no longer believed what he said. For the first time in my whole ordeal, truly and deeply, I started to fear for my life.

After we stopped and parked, Dessi joined us in the rear

section while Dr. Reyes stayed in the cab. Albert brought up a full-size image on the screen. I saw a field bordered by an overgrown grove of citrus trees. A car was parked in the field, dimly visible by the light of the moon. Albert then opened the ambulance door, and I saw a live version of the same sight. The car was sitting thirty meters away from us. It looked much clearer live, and I could tell right away what it was—my father's blue Mercedes.

I tried to control the trembling in my voice as I asked out loud, "Who is sitting in that car?"

Albert answered, "Ms. Meyers."

"Really? With the currency?"

He didn't answer.

I felt my throat go dry.

I watched Albert activate the split-screen function to bring in the scene at my house. He was not at all happy with what he saw: There was Mickie Meyers, my ex-stepmother, sitting at home in The Highlands. She was staring into the camera like she was about to begin a broadcast.

Albert actually gasped. "Wait a minute! Something is wrong." He turned on the audio button at our end, but not the video. Then he spoke in a harsh, raspy voice. "Ms. Meyers! What are you doing at home? You are supposed to be here. Didn't you read your instructions?"

If Mickie recognized his voice, she did not let on. She answered evenly. "We read your instructions, and we are co-operating. We have delivered the currency, all of it, in a trash bag, as instructed."

"We? Who?"

"Victoria."

I looked harder at the blue car in the field. I couldn't see anyone moving inside it.

Albert stammered, "The instructions were clear. You yourself were supposed to come."

Mickie shook her head. "The instructions were clear yesterday, too. Dr. Meyers came, and he lost his life. If anything goes wrong this time, Charity will still have one parent left alive."

At that moment, Dr. Reyes stepped into the back. He growled at Albert, "What is the delay?"

"The wrong person is here."

"What? Who's in the car?"

"Victoria. She sent the maid. Victoria."

"Does the maid have the currency?"

Mickie answered through the screen, "Yes, she does. All of it. And in the denominations you requested."

Dr. Reyes grunted. He told Albert, "All right. Then go get it."

I had never seen Albert so nervous. "That's not the plan. Ms. Meyers was supposed to come here. *That* was the plan."

Dr. Reyes dismissed his objections with a flick of his wrist. He answered, "So this is the new plan. Go."

After a tense moment, Albert got up and stalked out across the field, toward the car. As he did, the driver's-side door opened and I saw the white dome light reflect off Victoria's hair. She climbed out of the Mercedes, closed the door, and placed her own vidscreen on the car roof. Then she stood and waited for my kidnappers.

As soon as he got within five meters, Albert shouted, "Where's the currency?"

Victoria's eyes widened. Her hand shot to her mouth like

she had seen a ghost. She stifled most of a scream. Then, with a visible effort of will, she calmed herself enough to ask, "You? Albert? It's you?"

He answered brusquely: "Yes."

"How can this be? You—you work for RDS. You are part of the fam—"

Albert snapped, "It is me! That's all you need to know. It is me, and you need to give me the bag of currency. Now!"

Victoria pulled back, apparently afraid of what he might do. But she answered him in a strong voice: "I need to talk to you about that."

"No! No talking! Give me the currency now. You have your instructions."

Victoria raised her chin resolutely. "Yes, I do. From Ms. Meyers. Her instructions are that I need to see Charity before I give you the ransom."

Albert shook his head angrily. "No! Here's how it's going to work—"

Victoria cut him off, as if she were talking to a lazy repairman. "If you cannot show Charity to me immediately, I will need to speak to your boss. Where is he?"

Albert sounded flabbergasted. "What?"

"Your boss. The one who sent the instructions. Dr. Reyes. I'll talk to him now, not to you."

"That's not going to happen."

"Yes, it is. Or we are going to be standing here for a long time." They glared at each other for about twenty seconds, exchanging looks of pure hatred.

Finally, Dr. Reyes leaned toward my screen and growled at Victoria, "You heard what he said!"

"And you heard what I said. I will only do business with you."

Dr. Reyes threw up his hands. His eyes darted to the clock on the screen. "All right! I'm coming out there." He hurried to the doorway. I followed his jerky movements as he slid himself down to the ground and landed on an asphalt roadway. I leaned forward enough to look out and see that we were parked on a country road bordered by a shallow ditch.

Dr. Reyes started walking with difficulty, through the ditch and across the rutted field. As he did, I heard Albert break the silence with Victoria by asking the strangest question: "How did your father die?"

After a stunned pause, Victoria whispered, "What?"

"Your father. How did he die?"

"What are you talking about? What does my father—"

"What disease did he die from?"

I saw Victoria stick out her hands, speechless.

He persisted: "Just tell me and we'll move forward. Was it cancer?"

Victoria watched Dr. Reyes's slow progress for a moment. Then she answered quietly, "Yes."

"What kind?"

"Skin cancer. Melanoma."

"That is detectable by a simple screening. And it is one hundred percent curable if caught early. Remember that."

"Remember what?"

"That it is a curable disease."

She asked him, "Have you lost your mind?"

I was wondering the same thing. Dessi looked worried, too. He zoomed the lens closer. Victoria's face was a mixture of confusion and anger. She snarled at Albert, "Listen to you! What do you think you are, a doctor? You are nothing of the kind. You are a disgrace! That's all you are."

He replied, "Really? A disgrace to what? To fake English butlers in monkey suits?"

"No! A disgrace to human beings. To people who are what they say they are. To people who speak the truth."

"Oh? Is that right? So is your name Victoria? Are you a pretty little maid from Paris? Or is it London?"

"That is not my name, but I am an honest person! The things I say are true. I am not some phony, kidnapping liar. Some Dr. Jekyll and Mr. Hyde."

"You don't know who I am. After all these years, you have no idea."

"I know who you are now! And you'd better not have hurt that child!"

Dr. Reyes finally arrived, huffing, at the car. Without preamble, Victoria demanded, "I want to see Charity now. I want to take her away with me now."

Dr. Reyes answered breathlessly, "That is not the plan. You give us the currency. You drive away. We release the girl. That is the plan. The only plan."

"No. Ms. Meyers has instructed me *not* to give you the currency until I have seen Charity."

"Ms. Meyers is not giving the orders here! I am."

I watched mesmerized as Victoria, always a lady, did the most unladylike thing. She bent forward slightly and spat on the ground at Dr. Reyes's feet. "I am not afraid of you. None of you. You would abuse a helpless little girl? You deserve to die for that! If you bring her out here now, you can have your trash bag, and you can run away like pigs. Show me Charity. *That* is the new plan. Take it or leave it!"

Albert stepped forward menacingly, like he was about to slap her.

Dessi turned away from the screen. I could see the tension in his face. He placed his body in the frame of the doorway, his back to me, and spread out his arms and legs. He was now blocking my view, and my escape.

I had seen and heard enough. They were all losing it. Their stupid Plan B wasn't working. They knew they were going to be hunted down as murderers. They knew that I could identify them all, and testify against them all. Why would they ever let me go? Why would they ever let me live to be a witness?

I looked back at my vidscreen. At that exact second, Victoria took off running across the field! Albert turned and looked dumbly at Dr. Reyes, who barked at him, "Let her go! Look: the currency is there, on the front seat of the car."

Suddenly I knew what I had to do, too. Without a doubt. Victoria had shown me the way. I had to make a run for it—into the dark, into the night. I had to run for my life.

Dessi remained wedged in the ambulance door, his arms and legs splayed out before me like a large letter X. I crept forward to the bottom of the stretcher and lowered my feet to the floor. Then I dropped my right shoulder, took a deep breath, and launched myself at him, ramming him in the middle of his back.

Dessi's body bowed outward; then his fingers lost their grip and he pitched headfirst onto the asphalt. My momentum carried me to the lip of the open door, where I tottered

for a second and then fell forward, landing on my feet just behind the prostrate, gasping figure of Dessi.

I jumped over his legs and took off running to the left, down
the roadway. If Albert and Dr. Reyes hadn't heard me ramming
Dessi, then I had a few precious minutes to run for my life.

And run for it I did.

I'm not out of shape, but I'm not in run-for-your-life
shape, either. After about forty meters, my lungs started
burning; then my legs started cramping. I had to slow down; I
had to stop to breathe. I bent over, with my elbows on my
knees, and gulped for air. I was on the verge of throwing up,
but I didn't. I shook my head and my legs and my arms, trying
to revive my body for another sprint.

I looked to my right. I was just past the dirt field, at the
beginning of the citrus grove. I looked behind me. Dessi was
back up on his feet and running fast, faster than I ever could,
right at me. I took off again in a panic, running on sheer
adrenaline: running for my life.

Dessi caught me after ten more meters. He clapped a
hand on my shoulder and turned me around. This threw me
off balance, and I fell. I hit the asphalt and rolled downhill,
until I landed in the center of the ditch. I tried to scramble
back up, but I couldn't. I slipped and fell again, right on my
face, in some slimy weeds.

I looked up and Dessi was standing over me, panting and
sweating. He choked out the words, "Are you crazy? What are
you doing?"

I got up to a kneeling position. My eyes cast about for a
weapon—a rock, a stick, anything. I wasn't going to die without a fight.

Dessi gasped, "Dr. Reyes will kill you if you try to escape. Don't you know that?"

I clenched my fists and struggled to my feet. I snarled at him, "He'll kill me either way. No! This is my life! You're not going to take my life without a fight!"

He stretched his hands out, puzzled. When he spoke, it was a plea. "No. No, I'm not going to take your life. I never was."

"*Mantlè!* Liar!"

"No, I swear. That was never the plan."

"The plan? There's no plan! Did you plan to kill my father?"

Dessi's eyes widened. "No. Never. And . . . we didn't kill him. He killed himself. He was drunk."

"You did! You're guilty as sin. You're just as guilty as Reyes!"

"No. He doesn't tell me his plans."

"Right. Right. It's all on a need-to-know basis. Explain that, in pathetic detail, when you're on *Speakers' Corner.*"

"No. No, listen to me! Listen! I have my own plan."

"You? You have a plan? Mr. I Don't Know Crap?"

"Yes, I do. Ever since your father . . . got killed. I've been working this out in my mind. I am not a murderer."

"You're a kidnapper! It's the same thing."

"No, it isn't. Some kidnappers would go that far, yes. But I would not. Never. And they knew that." He jerked his head back toward the field. "From the beginning, the deal was that you wouldn't get hurt, in any way. I knew that much. We might make threats, but we were bluffing."

"Oh, right! Tell that to my father!"

"I swear! I swear that is true. And I'll prove it to you. I was going to let you go tonight no matter what. Even if Reyes said not to. Even if Monnonk said not to. I was going to find a way to set you free."

We both looked back at the field. The dome light inside the Mercedes was on again.

Dessi bent and looked in my eyes. "So you got *yourself* free. So let's keep going. I'll go with you; I'll help you."

I looked down the country road into endless darkness. I was desperate enough to ask him, "Where? Where can I go?"

He pointed at the row of trees. "There are houses down there, houses for the fruit pickers. Dozens of them. You can hide out in one. Then I'll call for help on the two-way."

I stared hard at Dessi, wanting to believe him. In the end, I had no choice. I said, "All right. Come on. Let's run."

Dessi jumped down and landed beside me. He cupped his hand under my arm. We climbed out the other side of the ditch and started running down a narrow path between rows of citrus trees. Both of us tripped and stumbled on the clots of dirt and the tall weeds, but we made steady progress.

Then we heard Albert's voice ringing sharp and clear: "Neve!" We froze until we realized the voice was coming through the two-way. "Neve! Where are you? Where's Charity?"

Dessi pulled the two-way out of his pocket. Albert continued, in a shrill tone, "Neve! Where are you? You better answer me, or you'll regret it!"

Dessi looked at me. "What should I do?"

I pointed toward a space between two trees. "Throw it in there. He might use it to trace us."

Dessi didn't hesitate. He flipped it away in a sidearm motion that sent the two-way crashing into the dark undergrowth.

Then we started running again. When we reached the end of the row, we found ourselves outside a circle of six wooden houses all resting on cinder blocks, all painted light blue.

Dessi stared at them for a moment, then decided: "No. Not enough cover. Not enough houses. Let's keep going." So we ran on, up a hill, to the edge of a blacktop road. "We're not very far from Mangrove," he told me. "We drove around for a while so you wouldn't know where you were. Do you think you can run for five more minutes?"

"Yeah. Yeah, I can."

We climbed up onto the roadway and turned left. I ran as hard as I could, two steps ahead of Dessi, who kept turning to check for the ambulance/truck. When he finally did see its headlights, he grabbed my arm and jerked me to the right. We fell and rolled down an embankment, crashing to a stop in some sharp branches.

Dessi whispered, "Keep your head down. Don't look at them, and don't move." The white truck drove by, slowly. When it was safely past us, he said, "We have to find a place to hide you, fast."

We struggled to our feet and looked around. A cluster of cement houses lay thirty meters to the right. We ran toward them. The houses appeared to be abandoned. Beyond them were some old trailers arranged in a haphazard line. Some of the trailers were inhabited. We could hear faint sounds coming from them, and we could see the blue glows of vidscreens.

Dessi said, "This will have to do. We'll hide you inside one of these empty houses. I'll check out the trailers. I'll find a friendly house that'll let me make a call. Okay?"

"Okay."

Dessi said, "Point to a house. Now! Don't even think about it."

I pointed to the fourth one. We ran to its front door and tried the knob. The door pushed open with a low creak. The light from the half moon peeked in through the door and through a cracked front window, but only for about three meters. The rest of the house was in complete blackness, like a monster's cave.

My eyes quickly adjusted to the low light, and it was not a pleasant sight. The house had been abandoned for so long that it was returning to nature. Weeds were growing up through cracks in the cement floor. Spiderwebs and animal nests filled every corner. I could not see bugs, or rodents, or other animals, but I could hear them scurrying.

Dessi whispered, "Stay away from the door and the window. Stay as far from the front as you can." I peered, terrified, into the blackness before me. He added, "I think I heard some Creole in that first trailer. Maybe they're my *frès*. Maybe they'll let me make a call. All right?"

I stammered, "All right."

"Are you okay?"

"Yeah."

"Okay. So I'm going now."

I grabbed his arm. "Listen, Dessi?"

"What?"

"I want to thank you."

"All right."

"And I want to tell you what I've been thinking."

"All right, but hurry."

"I was thinking that this is exactly what Ramiro would do."

"That's what you're thinking!"

"Yes."

"Well, start thinking about surviving; about keeping away from the front; about keeping your head down."

"Okay. All right." I lowered my head immediately and turned toward the back.

Then Dessi tried to leave, but he never got past the first step. I could feel him freeze just a meter away from me. Instinctively, I turned back to see what had happened. As soon as I did, I stifled a scream.

A big, menacing figure now stood before Dessi, blocking his getaway. And there was no question who it was—Albert.

Dessi stammered, "How? How did you get here?"

Albert raised one hand up and pointed at Dessi's U of Miami sweatshirt. He spoke calmly. "I'll show you. Empty your left pocket."

Dessi and I exchanged a hopeless look. Then he slowly obeyed. He held something up in his hand, something too small for me to see clearly.

Albert told him, "It wasn't hard to track you, Neve."

Dessi was suddenly outraged. "The GTD! You planted that on me! How could you?"

"Keep your voice down."

Dessi held the little ball bearing up. "This is what you think of me? This is how much you trust me?"

Albert spoke quizzically: "What are you saying? That you didn't lose your nerve? That you didn't just betray us and run away?"

"I thought this was about trust. And respect." Dessi threw the ball bearing at his uncle's feet. "This is not respect!"

Albert took one step back. He reached to his left and pulled in a bag from outside. A large black trash bag. Even in the dim light, I could see that it was packed to the ripping point with currency.

He held it out toward Dessi. "*This* is what it was about. And it's time to take your share."

Dessi now seemed on the verge of tears. "Oh, is that right? I thought it was about my mother, and you, and me." He took two steps forward and, with a karate-like kick, knocked the bag right out of Albert's hand. Wads of tightly bound multi-colored bills spilled out onto the cement floor.

I thought to myself, *That's what Ramiro Fortunato would have done, too.*

Albert leaned over calmly. He picked up the wads of paper and stuffed them back into the bag. Dessi and I exchanged another quick, desperate look. Did we dare to make a run for it? I backed a little farther into the house, looking for a possible way out through the blackness. I looked hard at the rear wall, but I could see nothing, not even a window.

When I turned around again, there was a second figure blocking the doorway.

Dr. Reyes had come up behind Albert. He was carrying a black bag, too, but it wasn't filled with currency. I knew what it was from the time I spent in my father's office. It was a doctor's emergency bag.

Albert stepped toward us. He spoke softly to Dessi. "Don't you understand, Neve? It's over now. We have succeeded."

Dessi spat back, "Succeeded?"

"Yes. Take your share of the currency. It's a small fortune. Take it and build yourself a new life."

Dessi's eyes flashed. "No!" He kicked at the bag again, but Albert pulled it away quickly. "No! I won't take one cent of it. And neither should you."

Albert set the bag on the floor behind him. He mumbled, "I'm sorry you feel that way."

"I do feel that way! We lied and robbed and killed to get that. We hurt innocent people. That money is poison!"

"No, it's not."

"Yes, it is! Don't you take it, either, Monnonk, or you will be damned. Do you hear me? You will be condemned to death, and executed, and damned to hell!"

Albert answered quietly, "I'm so sorry it came to this, Neve." His hands moved lightning fast. He grabbed Dessi by the left arm. Dessi tried to fight back, swinging his right arm and landing a glancing blow to the back of Albert's head, but it had no effect. Albert was too big and too well trained. He twisted Dessi around and pinned both his arms behind him. Then he forced him across the floor, toward Dr. Reyes.

Dr. Reyes reached into his medical bag. He held up a syringe in the moonlight. He tapped at the liquid within.

I screamed "No!" and launched myself at Albert. He turned himself so that I crashed with all my fury into his back and bounced right off.

I had no effect on him, either.

I screamed again, for all I was worth, but it didn't matter. Dr. Reyes calmly plunged the needle into Dessi's arm.

Dessi struggled for a few seconds, and then it was all over. I watched him fall lifeless to the floor.

Dr. Reyes put the needle back into the bag. With his free

hand, he took hold of Dessi's sweatshirt while Albert took hold of his feet. They dragged him just beyond the doorway, where Albert hefted his body up and bent it over his right shoulder. Then Albert carried him off.

All I could do was whisper, "Thank you for helping me, Dessi."

Dr. Reyes remained in the doorway, blocking my escape.

I knew that I was next. He would kill me next. What could I possibly do about it? Could I hurl myself through the front window? That would lacerate my face, but I might get through; I might hit the ground running; I might have a chance.

Dr. Reyes was staring at me. Hideous. Small. Evil. And I thought, *No, damn it. I'm not running from him to die beside the road like a stray dog. He's a common thief. A murderer. I am better than him.*

I dared to look him in the eye. I would not be cowardly at the end of my life; I would be defiant. I would be brave—like Patience, like Victoria, like Ramiro. I told him boldly, "So you got your trash bag, full of trash. Congratulations. That's all it is, you know. Dirty paper with dirty ink on it. It's trash. And so are you."

Dr. Reyes closed up his medical bag and laid it down. He took one step toward me and held out one hand in a "calm down" gesture.

I sneered, "So what are you going to do now? Reload and kill me? Or is Albert next? Is that it? A big surprise for Albert? You don't need him anymore. Will you stick a needle in him? Then me? Then everyone will be dead but you. And who are you?" I hocked up what little liquid I had left in my throat, leaned forward, and spat on the floor like I had seen Victoria do: "You are a small, ugly, evil man with a big bag full of trash."

He lowered his hand and, to my surprise, spoke. "Who am I?" He held both hands out. "I am a fellow passenger to the grave."

He straightened his back. It must have been a trick of the moonlight, but he actually seemed to grow taller in the process.

He peeled off his surgical scrub shirt and then his pants, revealing a white cotton T-shirt and blue jeans beneath. He reached his right hand up and, in swift, methodical gestures, pulled off his surgical cap and mask, his dark glasses, and finally a black wig.

Then he stood before me, immobile, daring me to believe my own eyes.

Oh my God, I thought to myself, too stunned to even whisper the words aloud. My whole body shook back and forth with one great spasm of shock, like I'd been standing in a field where they had tested a nuclear bomb.

My eyes widened and my mouth dropped open. For there before me, risen from the depths of Deep Lake, was my father, Dr. Hank Meyers.

After a long, long pause, I managed to whisper, "You . . . No. You're dead."

"No. Not dead. I'm alive."

"I saw you die. In the lake."

"No. You saw a helicopter crash."

"Your helicopter."

"My drone. With no one in it. My drone, made to look like

the real thing; shown from far enough away to look like the real thing."

I went on whispering, like I was talking to myself. "I saw you get in the real one. At the helipad."

"Yes, but you didn't see me get out. I landed it on the floodwall of Deep Lake. I put my shoulder under the fuselage, and I tipped the whole thing into the water. Then you saw me walk to the ambulance."

"No, I didn't."

"Yes, you did." He held up the Dr. Reyes mask and wig. "Dressed like this."

"But . . . But you couldn't have. You drove there with us, in the ambulance."

"No. I didn't. Neve opened and closed the door and made noise like I was getting in. But I wasn't there. He was up front alone."

I stood, working my jaw, for a full minute before I finally allowed the thought to get through. "You're not dead."

He dropped the costume to the floor. "To the rest of the world, I am. And I'm going to stay that way. But not for you. Not for you."

"Why?"

"I'll explain that soon. It'll take some time, though. For now, I just want to say I'm sorry. I'm sorry you had to think I was dead. I'm sorry you had to get so sick. I'm sorry for all that bad stuff."

I started babbling random words directly from my brain. "How? Why? What?"

Albert came back in, alone. He took one glance at my face and said, "It looks like you told her."

My father's voice answered, "I told her the basic fact. We need to talk at length, Charity, but not here. We can wait until we get back to the house."

A syllogism started running through my head: *People are either alive or dead. My father is not dead. Therefore . . .*

Albert picked up the trash bag full of currency and started out the door. I had no idea what to do next, so I followed him, walking zombie-like out to the waiting truck. Albert stashed the bag in the back. Then he and I climbed in. I sat on the front seat, while he slipped behind me and sat on a jump seat. I whispered, "Where's . . ."

Albert assured me, "He's on the stretcher."

"Is he dead?"

"No. He's fine. He's sedated."

"Are you lying?"

"No. No more lying."

My father climbed into the driver's seat.

Then the three of us rode in absolute silence back to the house in Mangrove.

Dr. Jekyll and Mr. Hyde

The half moon was still shining weakly on the old car and on the yellow walls of the house when we pulled up. Albert unclicked his seat belt and ducked into the back of the truck. After a minute, he called out, "His blood pressure's one fifteen over eighty."

My father answered, "That's good."

"Shall we leave him here?"

"Yes. Let's keep him in here, with the engine running. We'll keep an eye on him through the monitor."

My father then got out, so I followed. He led me through the screen door and into the living room, where he pointed to the recliner. "Why don't you sit there, Charity." He pulled up a red chair. "I'll sit in this one."

I hesitated, still too shocked to comprehend my situation,

but I knew I didn't want to sit down. I wanted to scream, but I held back.

I remained standing until Albert entered. For some reason, the sight of him released my anger. I snarled, "I guess your nephew was as stupid as I was! He believed in you, too!"

Albert looked at my father, and then at me. "I understand that you are very angry. And very confused as to why—"

"Angry?" I spat at him. "Do you really think 'angry' covers it?"

Albert shook his head no. He muttered, "For what it's worth, I am sorry."

My father added, "So am I. I—we are very sorry. We tried to make this as painless as possible for you."

I turned to him. "As painless as possible? I'm supposed to be grateful for that?"

His eyes showed hurt. He finally answered, "No."

I felt my anger surging like molten lava. "So . . . I'm supposed to thank you for poisoning me, for drugging me, for kidnapping me?"

"No. No—"

"For sticking me in front of a vidcamera and making me watch my own father's death? Making me react to it? Is that what this was all about? Did I look crushed enough for you? Did I cry enough? Was it a convincing performance? Did we fool Mickie?"

After a long pause, he finally admitted, "Yes. You're right, of course. That's what it was all about. You did convince Mickie. She firmly believes that I am dead. And you'll convince anyone else who ever sees that clip. Video doesn't lie."

Albert exchanged an uncomfortable look with my father,

then finally mumbled, "Okay. I'd better start packing the truck. Someone could be watching us; someone could be waiting to get their hands on that currency."

My father nodded. "Right. Do you need my help?"

"No. I'm only taking about half of this." Albert pointed to the equipment scattered around us. "Only what's in working order."

"All right. Set up what you can. I'll be down soon. Don't forget to paint the truck when you get there."

"I won't."

My father pointed to the chair again, but I just shook my head no. I stood and stared at the floor while he went about some final bits of business. He activated a small machine, a steel document shredder. I watched as he fed piece after piece into it—name tags, government IDs, papers. He also fed in the wig, followed by the surgical gloves and cap—all the props of their kidnapping plan. Finally he held up two items of mine—my red backpack and my footed pajamas—like he was asking my permission to dispose of them. I just looked away, so he stuffed those into the shredder, too.

Albert made about a dozen trips in and out with the medical equipment until the room was half cleared away. Then he hefted two trash bags.

As much as I hated to speak to Albert, I just had to know. I asked him, "So where did the second bag come from?"

Albert looked at my father for permission to speak. My father stopped his shredding to deliver the answer himself. "It came from our vault. It's all of our currency. I pulled it out of the Robinson before I tipped it into the lake."

"I see. So you actually got paid two ransoms?"

"Correct. The first one, supposedly, was destroyed."

"I see. So how much was I worth, exactly?"

He winced at that, then answered, "A whole lot. A fortune. Enough to let us do what we want to do."

I blurted out, "But you are a rich doctor! You already had all the money you could've possibly needed, ever, in a hundred years!"

He turned away from the shredder and stepped closer. "No. Dr. Henry Meyers did. He had enough money to be Dr. Henry Meyers for the rest of his days." He pointed at his own heart. "But that's not what *I* wanted."

I shook my head. "No. This is nuts."

"At first, Charity, yes. It seems nuts. That's why you have to sit down and listen to me. To hear me out."

I turned away, more determined than ever not to sit anywhere.

Albert made one final trip to the truck, then approached me in a manner that I would call, to use a Mrs. Veck word, sheepish. He said, "Listen, Charity: I don't blame you for hating me. Nobody deserves to be treated like that." He brought his big hand forward, and I looked at what he was holding. It was his leather chess set. "Nobody wants to be a pawn in the game, do they? Everybody wants to be a king or a queen."

I wasn't inclined to answer. He added, "But you can't play without that row of pawns. Can you?" After another silence, he answered himself. "Take it from me, you can't."

He finally turned to my father, saying, "Well, I'll see you down south," and left without another word. A minute later, I heard the All-Natural Organic Fertilizers truck back out and pull away.

At that point, I had to speak, because I had to know. "What's he going to do with his nephew?"

"Neve? He's going to leave him someplace safe."

"Abandon him, you mean?"

"No. I mean he's going to take him someplace and wait until he's all right. Then he's going to tell him what really happened."

"What really happened?" I scoffed. "You three were so screwed up, with your fake names and disguises and Plan B's, and your need-to-know basis. Do any of you even know what happened?"

My father answered, "Mostly. I'll tell you everything that I know in just a little bit. For now, be assured that Neve—"

"His name is Dessi."

That seemed to confuse him. "Really?"

"Yeah. And I'm not feeling too confident about what you know. You don't know the first thing about him. You don't even know his name."

"Okay. You got me there. But I know this: Albert will make sure that his nephew is all right—physically, financially, psychologically. Albert will tell him that we never killed anybody."

I felt a rush of pity for Dessi. He really hadn't known. He was just a pawn, too. I snarled, "Oh, isn't that kind of Albert. And of you." I glared at my father with real hatred. But my legs were now burning with exhaustion after that long run for freedom. I couldn't stand for another second, so I flopped into the red chair. My father walked around and sat in the recliner. Just sat. He didn't say anything.

I finally asked, wearily, "So what happens now? People

think you're dead. Do they think I'm dead, too? That we're both dead? Do we just sit here and act dead? Is that Plan C?"

"No. Of course not. There's so much I want to tell you. And the first thing is . . . that you're free now. Right now. Free to use the bathroom, or get a drink in the kitchen, or spit in my eye. Anything. All I ask is that you hear me out for a few minutes." He exhaled long and loud. He seemed exhausted, too.

I answered, "What do you have to drink?"

He smiled as best he could. "ElectroPlus. There are two bottles left in the refrigerator, a red and a blue."

I got up, half expecting this to be another lie, but it was true. I took the red one and carried it back to my seat. Then, from years of training by Victoria, I asked, "Did you want one, too?"

He smiled widely. After a long look at me, he said, "What a princess you are. Really. You are."

"Is that a no?"

"It's a no. I can't drink that stuff."

I sat down. "If I'm free to go now, when can I go?"

"In a few minutes, I'll drive you someplace safe, and Victoria can pick you up if you like."

"That sounds great. Provided it's true."

"It is true. I swear it is."

"You swear?" I scoffed.

"I swear on your mother's grave."

"My mother?"

"Yes. This is about you, and me, and her." He leaned forward and cupped his hands like he was holding a large ball.

"Remember how we used to live? With your mother? We were free. We had no walls, no security guards."

"I remember," I admitted.

He let the ball drop. "Then it all stopped. We moved into a prison called The Highlands. And you were like the princess in the tower. What's her name?"

"Who?"

"The princess."

"There are lots of princesses."

"The hair one."

"Rapunzel?"

"Yes. A princess locked in a tower. And that wasn't going to change, ever. Except maybe change for the worse. You wouldn't be the princess going to the ball, would you? You'd be the princess going to the guillotine."

"What are you talking about?"

"My . . . my fear for you. For us. And where life was leading us."

"Us? My life was fine. Talk about your own life."

"Yes. I will. Okay? Hear me out. This is what I wanted to say. Will you give me the chance?"

I took a deep swig of ElectroPlus. The taste flashed me back many years. I gave my father a gesture somewhere between a shrug and a nod, and he began:

"I don't expect you to follow all of this, Charity, you being so young. But after I married Mickie, I found myself trapped in a life that I could not stand. I got up every day and played a role that was not me. I was as fictional a character as Victoria and Albert. But they at least had a purpose for their act, didn't they? What purpose did I have? What did I actually do with my time? On a typical working day, I turned a rich woman with white skin into a rich woman with brown skin.

"I hated myself for doing that, but I continued to play that character—that DermaBronze playboy doctor. I guess I took a perverse sense of pleasure in playing someone I was not. Everyone was fooled. But deep inside, I felt nothing but pain. I was a sham. I was worthless. I did no good in my life.

"Then one day, on a trip to Miami, I happened upon a car accident. A child had been hit and left in the road. A hit-and-run. She was a girl just about your age. A woman and her son came running out of a house. They picked up the girl, which they shouldn't have done, and carried her across the street to another house. They yelled at some kids to go get the girl's family and bring them there, too.

"I watched all this, thinking, What does this have to do with me? I should just keep driving. But I didn't. Instead, I decided to break the pattern of my life; to do something that was not like me at all. I decided to help these people.

"I parked the car and walked up to the house. Everyone was chattering in Spanish. I understood that the house was a clinic, but the doctor was not in. I didn't hesitate. I raised my hands for silence. I told them all that *I* was a doctor. A real doctor. I set to work on that poor girl. It turned out she had a broken leg and contusions on her legs and arms, but nothing life-threatening. I had her in a leg splint and cleaned up in about twenty minutes.

"Well, you'd think I was the Second Coming of Christ! Suddenly the people were all around me, pumping my hand, hugging me, crying on my shirt. When I finally got free of them and started to go, I saw that a line of people had formed outside. They were waiting for that clinic doctor to return. A mother held a baby up to me and said, '*Ella está enferma.* She is sick.' What could I do? I went back inside and started acting like a damn doctor.

"Somewhere along the way, someone asked me my name. I thought up 'Reyes' on the spot. 'Reyes' for the Three Kings, because that's what I felt like. I added the *M.* later, just for fun. In one day, pretending to be Dr. Reyes, I helped over fifty people. These were people with serious problems—infections, sores, broken bones. I cured them all! I was so pumped up, so elated by the experience, that from that day on, I knew what I wanted to do with my life. With every remaining day of my life."

I must admit, I was fascinated by his speech. I never knew he had it in him. Or I knew it when I was little, but I had forgotten. Between the words of this caring, enthusiastic man and the retro sweet taste of the ElectroPlus, I felt like I was five years old again.

He aimed both pointer fingers at me; his eyes were shining. "Charity, think about it. All of our time, energy, and money go into keeping people away from us, into building up walls. What if we didn't do that? What if we became part of the world around us? What if we used all of that time, energy, and money for something else? For a greater good? We would no longer be people who were only worth a trash bag full of ransom money. We would be people who were worth something real. You and I, we could . . . redefine our lives; we could change them completely!"

He paused and waited for a reply. I didn't know what to say. Foolishly, I blurted out, "Can I use the bathroom?"

He sat back, disappointed, I think. He answered, "Of course, I said you could. So go ahead."

After I got up, he added tersely, "We could head out of here now, too. If you're ready."

"Yeah. Okay."

I laid my bottle down and hurried into the bathroom. I could hear him tidying up in the living room. What was going on with this strange man? I still didn't know if I could trust him. I still didn't know who he really was.

When I came out, he was standing by the kitchen archway. He had a small brown suitcase in his hand. "Ready?"

"Yes."

He led the way out the kitchen door. We crossed a patchy lawn to that old German car. It was a diesel hybrid of some kind, a two-door sedan with dark tinted windows. My father unlocked it manually. "Now, here's a car nobody would want to steal. It's very economical, though. It used to cost a fortune to run my 700D."

I got in the passenger side. The car smelled like tacos. I asked, "Where are we going?"

"To the turnpike. We'll stop at the rest area and talk a little more, if you're willing."

"Then what?"

"Then I will take off, in this car, to the south." He paused and added, "I hope . . . with you. But I will fully accept it if you choose to go back."

I *was* going back. I asked him, "How, exactly, will I get back?"

"Uh, you will call Mickie, or Victoria. I expect they will send Highlands security here to get you. I'll hide out and watch until you're safely in their custody, and then . . . I'll go."

After a few blocks, I asked him, "What's in the south?"

"That's where I live."

"That's where Dr. Reyes lives?"

"Yes."

"But you just shredded his identity, didn't you?"

"Yes. I've shut down his clinic, too. I've found a bigger space that I'll be moving to."

"As who? You can't be Dr. Reyes. You can't be Dr. Meyers."

"As someone new. A new version of me. Slightly older, I'm thinking." We pulled onto the Florida Turnpike ramp. "The clinic will have good diagnostic equipment. Refurbished, but good."

"Equipment supplied by Albert?"

"That's right. That's the plan."

"And you don't think anyone is ever going to find out who you are?"

"No. People down there have more important things on their minds. More important than a dead rich guy who couldn't fly a helicopter."

As we drove in his run-down Daimler alongside Ferraris and Peugeots and Porsches, he added, almost boisterously, "And you know what, Charity? I can't wait! I can't wait to get there and move in and set everything up and get started." Again, in a flash, I remembered my father the way he used to be, back when my mother was alive. He was boyish, and ideal-istic. He was someone to look up to.

We drove for about ten miles in silence except for the wheezing of that old car before he finally spoke again. "I said, on Christmas Eve, that you only get one chance to choose your path in life. I asked you to think about that. Did you?"

"No," I admitted. "Not really."

"Okay. Well, that's good, because it's not true. I was lying. You get as many chances as you want; as many as you dare to make for yourself."

We pulled off the turnpike and into the rest area. I looked at the long row of cars parked ahead of us and realized something: I was back in civilization. I was free to run to any one of these cars and knock on the window and announce who I was. I asked him, "Aren't the Highlands security guards looking for me now? And the police?"

"No. I don't think so."

"Why not?"

"Because your ex-stepmother knows what's good for her. She followed my instructions. She told the authorities exactly what she was supposed to tell them and nothing more."

We pulled into a diagonal space. I said, "You mean, Mickie did what was best for Mickie?"

My father shook his head sadly, but he spoke with a measure of forgiveness. "It's not her fault. It's mine. I never should have married her. I was so unhappy when I met her. I was like . . . a recluse. A hermit. All I did was work; you know that."

"You had no life."

"Not really. I was stumbling along, down the wrong path. And Mickie happened to be standing on it."

"Does she really think you're dead?"

"Oh yes. She's already filed a claim on my insurance."

"What about me?"

He looked down at the steering wheel. He spoke softly. "Obviously, if you call her tonight, she'll know you're okay. If you don't call her? I expect she'll draw her own conclusion, a limited conclusion based on what she saw on the vidscreen tonight and what she'll hear from Victoria."

I suddenly remembered the scene in the field. I warned him, "You'd better not have hurt her!"

"Who? Victoria? No! Heavens no. She ran away from us, and we let her run. She left the bag right there on the seat. We even waited for her to come back and drive away before we set off after you. She was fine."

"No, she wasn't fine! Not if she didn't have me! She was upset."

He cringed. "Yes. You're right. I don't know what I can say about that except, again, that I'm sorry."

"You used her like a pawn, too."

"I suppose we did, but that wasn't the plan. Mickie was supposed to deliver the currency."

The thought of Victoria driving home without me filled my eyes with tears. My father waited for a long time before adding, "Anyway, however this plays out, based on what we know about Mickie, you'll probably wind up as the subject of her next vidseries."

My anger at Mickie overtook my anger for him. "That's so phony! She doesn't care crap about me. How can she do that?"

"Because it's all just video to her. Mickie Meyers is what you see on the vidscreen. There's no one else in there. When the camera goes off, she ceases to exist." He shut off the engine. "Come on. We need to get you some solid food."

I nearly said, "That's what Mom told you once," but I stopped myself.

I followed him into the rest area's food court, a circular room of salad bars, SmartWater stations, and fast-food outlets. I half expected someone to point at me and yell, "That's the girl on the 'Taken' flyers!" But no one paid any attention to us.

We both ordered Mexican pizzas and liteshakes. I pointed out, "This will be my first solid food in three days."

My father grimaced. He picked up the tray and led the way to a clean table in the back with no other diners near it. He looked around to be sure no one was listening, then he began: "Do you remember what Victoria called Albert tonight, out in the field? Were you listening to that?"

"I was listening. But what? What did she call him?"

"Dr. Jekyll and Mr. Hyde! She called Albert that. And she was right, to some extent. But she should really have called *me* that."

"Victoria is always right."

"She is. Yeah. She's great."

We each took a bite and reflected on Victoria. Then he spoke again: "But it's really like the Jekyll-and-Hyde story in reverse. Dr. Henry Jekyll became an evil character, Edward Hyde. Edward Hyde grew ever stronger and took over the life of the good but weak Henry Jekyll.

"For me, the opposite happened. Every time Dr. Reyes appeared at the clinic and helped heal wounds and stop infections and save lives, he became stronger. And Dr. Hank Meyers, hiding behind his walls, hoarding his currency in his vault, became weaker. Soon I was actively plotting how to escape into Reyes full-time. I made Hank Meyers into even more of a selfish buffoon, with the golf and the helicopter and the college football. The more self-indulgent Hank Meyers became, the less chance there was of anyone relating him to the selfless Dr. Reyes.

"Then one day Albert came walking into my clinic, in regular clothes, of course. He had brought his sister there for help. I froze when he looked at me. I thought my double life had been exposed and all would be destroyed. But Albert had a secret of his own. He had lied to get medical coverage for his sister, and he was in a lot of trouble with RDS."

I said, "I actually know this part. Dessi told me."

My father looked confused again; then he remembered. "Oh. Right. Neve."

"Sorry. Go on."

He collected his thoughts. "Okay. RDS contacted me about firing Albert, but I said no. Instead, Albert and I made a deal. I would protect his lie, and he would protect mine. And I would give his sister the best medical care I could." His eyes widened. "Then, just on his own, on his days off, he started to help out at the clinic, too! He assisted with the more complicated procedures, like the cleft palate surgeries."

"As Dr. Lanyon?"

He looked amazed. "Yes. How did you know that?"

"I just figured it out. Dr. Lanyon was another name that you used. Dessi used it during the kidnapping. So if Albert used it during a cleft palate surgery, a girl who wanted to thank him with a *tornada* would carve an *L* on it."

He pointed at me. "That's very good. Yes. He showed me that doll. He was proud of it." His voice rose. "Of course he was! What else did he have to be proud of? Trimming Mickie's damn Christmas tree? Washing my car? No. Albert plunged

219

into the new life just like I had, full tilt." His voice dropped. "And that's when the kidnapping plot was born."

I held up a hand to stop him. "That's what I can't understand. Why did you have to attack me like that? Your own daughter." He looked wounded. I added, "Why couldn't you just divorce Mickie, move out with me, and open your own clinic down south?"

He pressed his pointer fingers together. "Because we wouldn't *belong* there, and people would know it. There are bad people down there, Charity. Lots of them. Bad poor people. Poor doesn't equal good, believe me. They'd go after a wealthy doctor and his daughter. We would never have been safe."

He rolled his eyes. "And your ex-stepmother? Would she ever leave us alone, with a story like that to tell? No. I knew I had to give Mickie *another* story, and now she has it. Her husband is dead; her stepdaughter has been taken. She'll run with that one for years."

A noisy family of four sat at the table next to us. My father leaned forward and whispered, "The final, ultimate question was: Could I leave Dr. Henry Meyers behind forever? And the answer was, I could, except for one thing—my daughter. You. I wanted you to have the chance to join me, Charity. To join me in the kind of life that we once had, where we were free. That's what this was all about. And, as crazy as it might sound, I think it was the right thing to do."

He sat back, as if he had rested his case.

Now it was my turn to reply. He wasn't going to like what he heard. "Okay. Thank you for the explanation. But . . . what you did was outrageous, and dangerous, and it did hurt a lot of people. Look at Dessi. Look at Victoria. As to the clinic doctor business, I think you should do it if it makes you happy. But it's not for me. I have friends. I have school. I have Victoria."

He replied, with an edge of desperation, "But you'd go to school. I have one in mind. It's a Catholic school with real kids, not vidscreen kids."

"What? I would go to school disguised? Like at Halloween? That's nuts. That's no way to live."

"Listen! Listen. You forget who I am. I have a unique ability. I can change the way people look almost permanently. You could change your appearance and never have to worry about being recognized. You could have fun with that—choosing your new hair and eyes and all. You could change your name! I already have one for you. Listen to this: Caridad. 'Charity' in Spanish is *caridad*. You'd be Cari, and I'd be Dad."

He smiled a heartbreaking smile at me. Heartbreaking because it was not going to be returned. I shook my head back and forth and whispered, "No. It's a crazy plan. You should never have done this to me. My answer is no."

We sat in miserable silence until he managed to say, "All right. Well, thank you for listening. And again, I am sorry." A tear bubbled up in the corner of his right eye and rolled down his cheek. "You remember when you made that plea into the vidcamera, when you asked me to please help you? I was sitting in the house, just ten meters away, and I was answering you back. 'I am,' I said. 'I am helping you.' But I guess I was wrong."

"Yes," I told him. "You were wrong."

He wiped his eyes with a napkin. "Maybe you'd like some time to think—"

"No."

He folded the napkin carefully and set it down. "Okay, then. I'm sorry again. Just tell me when you're ready to go."

"I'm ready right now."

"Okay."

"Okay."

As I stood up to leave, though, my mind began racing, like when I first came to my senses after the kidnapping. I shook my head to clear my thoughts. I was ready to go home to The Highlands. That's all I had hoped for since the ordeal began. I was ready to go back. Wasn't I?

After we had walked through the food court, I surprised my father with a question. "What did it say in Rockefeller Center? About useful service?"

He smiled curiously, and sadly. "You remember that?"

"Yeah. What was it?"

" 'The rendering of useful service is the common duty of mankind.' "

"Yeah. And the part about selfishness burning up, and—what's the rest?"

He held the door open and told me, " 'The greatness of the human soul is set free.' "

"Yeah."

We stepped back out into the cold air. The moon was gone. The stars were shining brightly all around me. I stepped off the sidewalk into the wide parking lot and looked down. I was standing on top of a yellow line. It ran from my feet across many meters of asphalt and off into the darkness, into infinity. It was a thick line, cracked in many places, stained with tire marks and oil spots—the line that separated northbound traffic from southbound traffic.

Those were my two choices.

Northbound was life with Mickie and Victoria. Southbound was life with my father and, in a way, the ghost of my mother.

I stood on that line for what seemed like a long time, looking both ways. I thought about everything that had brought me to that point. I went back over what I had learned about myself in the last two days. And I thought about what I wanted to do with the rest of my life.

El Día de los Reyes

My father pulled the old Daimler into a dirt field. It was not a great parking spot, but we were both happy and relieved to be out of the car after the long drive from Miami.

We walked quickly toward the clamor of activity and excitement at the center of town, a celebration advertised by a red-and-white banner that spanned the main road: LA IGLESIA DE LA NATIVIDAD WELCOMES YOU TO THE TOWN OF MANGROVE'S CHRISTMAS CARNAVAL, JANUARY 6, 2036.

We turned left at the banner and began a slow progress through the crowd: people dressed in wild, feathery costumes; people waving brightly colored lanterns; people squirting water at each other from plastic pistols.

Up ahead, I could see the stage lights and other preparations for a Mickie Meyers vidcast. Mickie and her crew had set up, once again, in the town center of Mangrove. I could see her standing with the mayor and Mr. Patterson on a short riser while an assortment of kids-to-be-used-as-props flanked the stage. The Highlands kids, with their lighter derma, occupied the area to the right. The Mangrove kids stood to the left.

We veered left, and I walked right through the Mangrove kids as if I were one of them, as if I had always been one of them. From behind, I heard my father whisper, "Don't get too confident now, Cari."

I smiled a perfect white smile. "I won't, Papi."

As before, a large vidscreen had been set up on the side of the stage. Until the show began, a stationary camera on top of the screen was scanning the faces in the crowd. I moved forward carefully until I could see both my father and me on it. My father had very dark skin, and the white hair and white bushy mustache of an elderly Hispanic man. He looked somewhat hunched, as if he'd spent a lifetime picking lettuce. (He did not look that way in his clinic, though, as Dr. Nueves.)

I looked more like his granddaughter, *su nieta,* than his daughter, *su hija.* I had a government ID card that said I was Caridad Nueves. It was a hortatory name, the same one my mother had given me. My straight brown hair was gone—it was now curly and black. My eyes were a deep brown to match it. My derma was three shades darker than it had been, too. I was wearing a Guatemalan corte jacket with deep pockets, and balsa-wood clogs that made me look ten centimeters taller. In my opinion, the girl on the vidscreen looked very much like Victoria.

I turned to watch the broadcast preparations. Lena

hurried past me without so much as a glance. Then Mickie herself, while checking out the crowd, looked right at me. Clearly, she did not recognize me. Or my father.

I whispered, "Papi, Mickie doesn't know you."

He grinned. "No, Cari. She never did."

Mickie's attention switched to the two men standing next to her—Mayor Ortiz and Mr. Patterson. I edged close enough to hear her ask the mayor, "Why couldn't you have started this party one hour later? Or moved it one street over?"

The mayor shrugged. "We only have one main street. And the Carnaval starts when the church says it starts. I have nothing to do with it."

"Wouldn't the church listen to you? Aren't you the mayor?"

"I am. I am the mayor of Mangrove, which today is having its Christmas Carnaval as it does every year on El Día de los Reyes. If you want to do a show about that, you are more than welcome."

Mickie shook her head angrily. "The show isn't about that. It's about my stepdaughter. My kidnapped stepdaughter. Don't you know that?"

"Oh, I know it. She was taken from home, was she not, from The Highlands? With its great security? That would be an interesting show to see. And you could vid it right there, in The Highlands."

Mickie pointed at the ground. "This is where she was held prisoner. In Mangrove. This is where the kidnappers lived."

The mayor smiled slightly. "I don't know about that. I heard it was an inside job."

Mickie snarled. "All right. Forget it. Forget you. You're never going to see your face on my show again, ever." The mayor raised his eyebrows, indicating that he didn't much care, which made Mickie even angrier. She went on: "And there will be no more Kid-to-Kid Days, either."

The mayor smiled. "They really weren't worth all the trouble for us. The extra security; the trash pickup. And then, most of our kids refused to wear those clothes anyway."

Mickie opened her mouth to say something angry, but she never got the chance. A reveler in green sequins and pink feathers danced up beside her, raised a water pistol, and blasted her in the back of the neck. Mickie screamed like she had been shot by a bullet. She yelled, "My God! Lena! Get over here!" Then she ducked behind the line of bemused Highlands kids and started haranguing the security guards: "Did you see that? What if that was a real gun! I'd be dead now." The guards, followed by the butlers, pulled out their Glocks. They aimed them at the feathered people in the crowd, who just laughed and squirted water at them.

I found a place about five rows back from the stage and waited, with about one hundred others, for Mickie to calm down, dry off, and begin the vidcast. The large screen went blank for a moment and then flickered on again with Mickie's logo—a pair of rectangular red glasses beneath which, as if written by an invisible hand, appeared the name Mickie Meyers in lipstick-red cursive. Then the logo faded away and a new image appeared.

I stared at the vidscreen for several seconds before I could comprehend this fact: I was looking at myself, my old self from just one week before. My pale, unsmiling face, in grainy black-and-white, now filled the bottom two-thirds of the screen, while information about my kidnapping filled the top third. This was the "Taken" flyer that Patience and Hopewell had created and passed out all over Mangrove, at risk to their own lives. With my jaw hanging open and my lips moving slightly, I read the words: "Taken, January first, two thousand thirty-six, from The Highlands."

The flyer then started to fade, and a live image of Mickie's face filled the screen. She stared into the camera, rather grimly, and said, "This is Mickie Meyers, reporting from the town of Mangrove, a town sometimes associated with revelry and fun. But recently, it's a town associated with a heinous crime—the kidnapping of my stepdaughter, Charity Meyers, and the murder of her father, Dr. Henry Meyers. The flyer that you just saw is part of a continuing effort to find Charity Meyers. That effort goes on, as I will explain to you later in the broadcast."

Mickie followed Kurt and his camera to the center of the stage. "First, though, I would like to begin with a very special story. Isn't it always at times like these, when evil seems to be winning, that a hero emerges? That's exactly what happened here. Let me open this segment by reading a passage to you from one of the most popular novel series of the last ten years, brought to you by SatPub. I am, of course, referring to the Ramiro Fortunato Series for Young Readers."

Mickie held up a familiar-looking book and started to read out loud: " 'Even though we needed the currency badly to fix a hole in the roof, I returned the bound-up wad of dollars to the elderly couple. They were so grateful. They called me a hero. But no, I wasn't a hero. I was just someone trying to do what was right.' "

Mickie closed the book dramatically and explained, "The

speaker is a young man named Ramiro Fortunato. In this series of books, he faces many challenges, some of them dangerous, but he always triumphs because he knows what is right. And he *does* what is right. But don't just take my word for it."

Mickie stepped down from the stage and walked into the crowd. At first I was shocked by such an un-Mickie-like move, and I started to back away. But I soon figured out that it was prearranged; a group of kids had been hand-selected to talk to her. Mickie extended the microphone and asked the nearest girl, "What is your favorite Ramiro story?"

The girl leaned toward it shyly and replied, "The one where he saw a lawn guy rob a kid's bike and throw it in a van. Ramiro ran after the van so fast that he caught the guy and made him give the bike back."

"Good," Mickie replied. "Great."

She turned to a short boy. "How about you?"

The boy smiled slyly. "Uh, I like the one where Ramiro Fortunato gets into a fight with a drug dealer."

"Yes? Really? Go on."

The boy went on. "Yeah. And he kicked his lily-white ass."

The rest of the kids snickered. Mickie pulled back the mike. She muttered to Lena, "At least we're not live." Kurt set up next to her, the light came on, and she continued. "Like these children, one boy from this town grew up loving Ramiro Fortunato novels. He took them to heart. Then, one week ago, he had the opportunity to become a hero himself. You are going to meet that very special young man today."

Mickie climbed back onto the stage, talking as she went. "You all know by now what happened to Dr. Henry Meyers and his daughter, Charity. It was a tragedy that struck close to the heart for me. And I want to thank all of you for your prayers and for your messages of hope."

Mickie paused and looked upward. Even from my spot, some ten meters away, I could see her eyes moisten. As if on cue, tears rolled down her cheeks. They looked positively enormous on the vidscreen, like an avalanche of phony grief. Mickie gulped audibly and then continued: "It was especially moving to hear from parents who have gone through such a tragedy themselves, and who are still going through it. Still 'living with it,' as I am.

"What you might not know is the role a young man from Mangrove played in a daring rescue attempt. He did not succeed, but he did try. He did what he knew was right. And that's why he is a real-life Ramiro. Let me introduce you to a young man who just wants to be called Dezi." She turned to Lena and added rhetorically, "His mother must have been a big *I Love Lucy* fan to call him that. Right? Let's bring him out."

I couldn't believe my ears. I looked around and caught my father's eye. He raised his shoulders, as puzzled as I was.

At Lena's urging, Dessi walked out from the side of the stage and stood next to Mickie. He looked terrified. I saw no trace of the anger, or the arrogance, that usually showed on his face.

Mickie took him by the elbow. She began by mispronouncing his name again: "Dezi, first of all, thank you for what you tried to do for me and my family."

Dessi didn't correct her pronunciation. He just answered nervously, "You're welcome."

Mickie held up her book. "Tell me, Dezi, when did you

start reading Ramiro Fortunato novels? Was it as a child, as I've been told?"

"Yes."

"Did your mother read them to you?"

"Well—"

"And then she died, tragically, leaving you those memories of reading together, didn't she?"

Dessi shifted uncomfortably. "Sort of."

"So, Dezi, I'd like you to tell the audience now, in your own words, what you did to become a real-life Ramiro."

Dessi flinched as the mike was thrust in his face, but he did speak up. "I tried to help the girl who was taken. You know. Your daughter."

"My stepdaughter, Charity Meyers. Yes. An upcoming series of shows will be dedicated to finding her and to bringing her home. Now, tell us how you risked your life trying to rescue her from a gang of kidnappers. They were armed and dangerous, weren't they?"

"Yes. They had Glocks."

"Glock semi-automatic machine guns?"

"Right. They were searching in a grove for something, or somebody. I thought that looked strange, so I investigated."

"As Ramiro might have done."

"Then I saw a girl hiding. She begged me to help her, so I did."

"And that girl was my stepdaughter, Charity Meyers?"

"Yes."

"So what did you do next?"

"I told her, 'Come on, I know where we can get help.' And

we started running. We found some abandoned houses to hide in. But—but they caught us."

"And what did they do when they caught you?"

"They knocked me out. I thought I was dead. But then I woke up in a house, and . . . I wasn't dead."

Mickie turned and looked purposefully at the mayor. "And that all happened right here in the town of Mangrove, didn't it?"

"Yes."

"So you risked your life to help this girl. You didn't even know her, did you?"

"No."

"So why did you do it?"

Dessi hesitated for just a moment before answering, "Because it was the right thing to do."

Mickie lowered the microphone and looked at the audience. The people started to clap warmly. Mickie talked over the sound. "That's the kind of heroism, the kind that asks for no reward, that he learned from the Ramiro Fortunato series of novels. And that is precisely why we think he *does* deserve a reward." The people applauded louder. "And the folks at SatPub agree, Dezi, which is why they are giving you this: a complete set of Ramiro Fortunato novels, hardbound. What do you think of that?"

Dessi didn't answer. He just shifted from foot to foot.

Mickie went on. "But that's just the start of it, Dezi. When we were talking earlier, what did you tell me that you wanted to do with your life?"

"I said I wanted to be a doctor."

"To be a clinic doctor."

"Well, to be a doctor."

"A doctor who runs a clinic that helps poor people like you."

"That helps people like my mother."

"Okay. Well, you might need a doctor yourself when you hear about this next gift. We are presenting you today with what college administrators call 'a free ride.' Based on your very impressive high school transcript, you will receive a full scholarship—tuition, room, meals, books—to the University of Miami."

The audience broke into spontaneous applause. Dessi turned to the crowd and smiled shyly. His eyes started filling with tears.

Mickie continued, "You'll be majoring in pre-med, I take it."

He nodded, clearly overcome with emotion.

"And you're going to work very hard?"

He managed to choke out, "Oh yes."

"Because, Dezi, there is a catch. We're going to be checking in on you from time to time. Is that okay?" She waited for a reaction. When there wasn't any, she went on. "If you can maintain a three-point-five average, your free ride will continue right through medical school. What do you have to say about that?"

The applause started up again. Dessi spoke over it. "I say thank you. Thank you very much." He pointed to the sky. "And thank God."

"Yes indeed. Now what might your mother say about all this?"

"My mother would be very happy. And my father."

"Happy that their son was a real-life Ramiro Fortunato."

Dessi tried to say something else about that last comment, but Mickie had already turned away and was addressing the camera. "Still, as you know, Dezi's heroic actions could not prevent this tragedy. Charity Meyers was taken away by those kidnappers, a vicious band who also murdered her father in the process. Where is she now? We do not know. When we return, I'll speak to some of Charity's classmates to ask them how they are coping with this tragedy."

Lena herded "my classmates" onto the stage. Dessi tried to step off, but Lena hissed at him to stay in place. Then I saw a young woman in the crowd with long, lustrous hair. She was standing to the right of the stage. Dessi bent down to ask her something, and she replied.

It was Victoria. Why on earth was *she* speaking to Dessi?

I puzzled about that as I watched the Dugan sisters clomp onto the back riser. They were followed by Sierra, Patience, Hopewell, and Sterling Johnston. Lena must have been distracted by all the water squirters, because she allowed Sterling Johnston to stand in the front. Apparently, he was still taking his medication.

As soon as they were all in place, Kurt the cameraman positioned himself in front of Mickie and she began: "A young child, just like these children standing behind me, is taken by ruthless kidnappers. What will happen to her? Let's ask some of her classmates what they think. Sierra, do you believe you will see your classmate Charity again?"

At first, Sierra didn't answer. But when the microphone remained in front of her, she muttered, "I don't know."

Mickie tried again: "Who does believe we will see Charity again, that we will get her back where she belongs?"

I watched with pride as Patience and Hopewell raised their hands.

"That's right. So do I. And because I do, I want to address Charity directly." I froze, but I quickly realized that Mickie was not looking at me. She was looking at Kurt. I met her gaze on the big vidscreen. "Charity, honey, I feel in my heart that you are still alive. I want you to know that we, meaning the crew and I and the people from GlobalKidSearch, the most successful victim-retrieval agency in the United States, are determined to find you. As soon as we leave here today, we are heading to South America. Could you have been taken there? To Brazil? To Argentina?"

Mickie backed up toward the Highlands kids in order to make her final remarks. "I intend to find out where you are, whatever it takes. I pray that we may have a glorious reunion show someday." She paused and concluded, "But for the present, and for the near future, we will all be 'living with the uncertainty' of not knowing." The red light blinked off, and Kurt lowered the camera.

As the people in front of the stage dispersed, my father slipped into the space next to me. "*Mi hija,* what did you think of all that?"

I answered with a whispered syllogism: "All Mickie Meyers specials are stupid. This was a Mickie Meyers special. Therefore, this was stupid."

"Yeah. If she only knew how stupid, huh?"

His eyes twinkled merrily behind his old-guy disguise. I had to smile. But then I told him seriously, "You know why I'm really here, Papi. There's someone I have to see."

He nodded. "I know. You can go talk to her, but you must be very careful."

"I will be."

"We'll have to be getting back soon, Cari. There's much work to be done."

"Sí, Papi." I stood for a few more minutes, watching as my classmates left the stage. I noticed that Whitney was not among them. I figured that her family wouldn't let her leave The Highlands, not even in the security van. All the other Amsterdam Academy students were there, though, looking miserable, especially against the backdrop of the laughing, singing revelers.

Victoria's words came into my head: "You need to live life, Miss. You need to have adventures." Patience's feisty spirit came into my head, too, and I decided to have an adventure. I walked right up to Sierra and the Dugans as they stood together, silently picking at threads in their plaid jumpers like uniformed orangutans. They did not seem to notice me. I stopped in front of Pauline Dugan and smiled. She didn't even look up. I spoke to her anyway: *"Tu hermana es mierda."*

"Huh? Hey, Sierra, what's she saying?"

Sierra sneered widely. "I don't know."

Maureen added, "Tell her to get lost, Sierra."

"I told you! I don't speak Spanish."

"Yeah. Right."

I pointed at each of them in turn and told them, *"Tú, y tu amiga, y tu hermana son mierdas. ¿Comprende?"*

All three turned their backs. But before they did, Maureen snarled, "Hey, go tell it to the lawn guy."

I smiled pleasantly and walked on, to my true destination. Victoria was still standing to the right of the stage, where I had last seen her. I walked up and just stood for a moment. Then I pulled a small orange from my pocket and held it out for her to see. I whispered, in my best Spanish, *"¿Quiere usted una naranja?"*

Victoria looked at the orange, and then at my hand, and then at my face. Her own face turned white with shock. She gasped out loud, *"¡Madre de Dios!"* and made the sign of the cross.

I wanted to say something else, something comforting, but she pushed past me and hurried off, walking in a strange, tilting way, like she was about to fall on her face. I followed her away from the crowd. She finally stopped next to a thick oak tree, leaned against it, and started to pray, *"Ave María, gratia plena . . ."*

I waited until she finished the prayer to say, "I am so sorry, Victoria. I know this is a great shock."

She kept staring at the ground. *"Milagro. Es un milagro.* It is a miracle."

"I'm sorry to scare you. But I had to see you."

"I prayed for this moment. And it has come true."

"Yes."

"I prayed that you would appear again."

I answered softly, "And I have."

Victoria closed her eyes. *"Madre de Dios.* When I was in the field that horrible night, I prayed and prayed to God. I said, 'Tell me if she is hurt.' When I heard nothing back, it gave me hope."

She finally looked at me, her eyes flowing with tears, and whispered, "Oh, Miss." She hugged me tightly to her for a long time. I melted away in her arms and cried, too, until she finally said, "I have never prayed so hard for guidance from God. From the Virgin Mary. From all the saints. I was so worried."

"I was worried about you, too. What happened to you that night?"

"To me? Nothing."

"You were so brave."

She shook her head. "Me? Oh no." She explained, "Ms. Meyers said not to give them the ransom until I saw you. But those men would not let me see you. So I was stuck. The only way out was to run. That way they could take the bag themselves, but I had not given it to them. See?"

"Yes. I see. So what did Mickie say when you got back?"

"She asked me what happened, and I told her the truth: 'They took the bag.' She said, 'Where's Charity?' I said, 'I don't know.' And that was that. She never asked anything else."

I cast a quick look around and saw my father waiting by the stage. I whispered urgently, "I had to see you again. I wanted you to know I was all right. But I'm sorry, I can't stay long and I can't answer any questions."

Victoria tried to follow my gaze. She wiped the tears from her eyes with two quick swipes. "Do you mean questions like, Are you well? Are you sleeping? Are you living life?"

I laughed in spite of myself. "Yes. Like those."

"I will try."

"Okay. But would you answer some for me? Please? There are things I need to know."

Victoria nodded. She leaned her back against the tree and took several deep breaths. When she spoke again, she was calm. She said, "Let me tell you this first: I tracked that boy down who tried to help you. That Dessi. It's Dessi, right? With *s*?"

"Yes. How did you ever find him?"

"Through Patience Patterson. She told me about a boy who they met in Mangrove. He broke up a fight between Patience and Hopewell and some others. He sounded like the boy I saw in the door of the kidnappers' truck that night."

"You saw him?"

"Yes, very clearly."

"I was right behind him!"

She shook her head sadly. "Oh, Miss, I am so sorry."

"No. No, don't be. Go on."

Victoria pointed toward the town center. "The next day, I drove to Mangrove, to where that fight happened. I asked around. I figured that people who would never talk to Patience, or to Hopewell, or to you"—she smiled—"to the *old* you, would talk to me. And they did! A woman told me about a tall boy with dark skin who was working at a clinic. I found him that day, and I had a long talk with him."

I snorted. "You mean, he had a long talk with you?"

"What?"

"Wasn't he arrogant?"

"No. Not at all. He was very sad, and sorry, and frightened. He told me what happened that night. Everything that he could remember." Victoria looked back toward the stage. "I told some of it to Ms. Meyers. And she made up the rest."

"Yeah. I know. I heard the broadcast."

"Dessi said you were still alive, but he didn't know too much more. He said everything was on a need-to-know basis, and he only knew what that Albert creep told him, or something like that."

Victoria looked around, as if contemplating spitting on

the ground again. "I wanted to have Albert arrested, you know." She leaned toward me and whispered, "But Ms. Meyers did not. I am not sure why, but Albert always said that she was stealing currency from your father." She straightened up again and spoke aloud. "Anyway, when I finished hearing what Dessi said about you, and how he had tried to help you, you know who I thought of."

"Ramiro Fortunato."

"Yes! I told Ms. Meyers that part. And I told her about Dessi wanting to be a doctor. And that's why he got the scholarship. It's like the end of a Ramiro story."

A band of revelers danced past us and aimed some water our way. They wet our legs and shoes, but Victoria just smiled at them. I reached into my other pocket. "Before I go, will you do me a favor? *Por favor?*"

"*Sí.*"

I pulled out two *tornada* dolls—one carved with a *P;* one carved with an *H*. "These are for friends I will see again someday—Patience and Hopewell. The dolls will speak for themselves. Patience will know what they mean. Hopewell will, too, I'm sure."

I held them waist high for her to see. "And, if you feel like having some fun, you could tell Patience that the *H* one is really for her. It stands for 'hor.'" Victoria frowned. "It's a joke. A private joke," I assured her.

"It's not so private, Miss. I know how you two joke around. Bad girls."

"Sorry. Forget that part."

Victoria took the dolls from me and slipped them into her coat pocket. "I'll let *las tornadas* speak for themselves."

I looked over at the stage. Patience, Hopewell, and the others were standing in a tight pack, surrounded by guards. Mickie and Dessi were talking to the mayor. Lena was behind them with an umbrella, trying to deflect the streams of water still being aimed at Mickie. I asked Victoria, "What did Mickie do when she got the instructions from the kidnappers? Did she consider calling the police?"

"No. She followed the instructions to the letter. Right from the beginning. Even after your father got killed, even after you disappeared, she still followed the instructions. After we switched to Plan B, she called the police and read a statement to them, word for word, just like it was written by the kidnappers. Then she shredded all of the instructions."

"So . . . does she think I'm dead?"

"No. I told her that I think you're alive. She believes that. She thinks your father is dead, of course." Victoria paused to study my reaction. "And, of course, he is, officially. Right?"

I answered carefully, "Yes. He is officially dead," and I changed the subject. "Is Mickie really going to look for me?"

Victoria kept staring at me for ten seconds. Then she answered, "Yes. In her way. She's flying to Rio and Buenos Aires to shoot some video. She's saying that you may have been sold to a wealthy family down there."

"Yeah? As what? As their maid?"

Victoria smiled. "Yes, I suppose." We both glanced over at Mickie. She was standing alone now on the center of the stage, with a blank expression on her face. Victoria told me kindly, "She doesn't think too hard about things, Charity. Not like you and I do. This kidnapping was way too much for her."

I liked hearing her say my name without the Miss, even if

it was my old name, my past name. I answered, "Right. So what will you tell her about today?"

"That's up to you. Do you want her to know that you're okay?"

"No. Don't ruin her show. I'll be the missing child in South America. It doesn't really matter to me. Not anymore."

Victoria nodded solemnly. "I have to ask you one thing, though: Are you having any bad dreams?"

"No. Not one. Not since I left The Highlands."

"Really?"

"Not even when I was a prisoner."

She seemed to look within herself. "That's very interesting. I'm glad to hear it."

I told her, "So now you can get some sleep."

"Yeah. I'll need it. Now that I've given my notice."

"What?"

"I've quit RDS."

"Really?"

"Sure. Why would I stay? The house is sold. There's no one to take care of."

"You mean, there's no one to follow to school because she forgot her lunch?"

"Right. And what about that, Charity? What about school? Where will you go?"

"I'm set to go to a Catholic school. I can't tell you where, though. Okay?"

"Yes. I understand."

"I'll go to high school there, too, and then I'll go to college. Like you."

"Yes. You should."

"Do you know where you'll be going?"

"I do. To Barry University. I have saved enough money for four years of college there, and then three years of law school, if I'm frugal."

I smiled my old manipulative smile at her. "I see. And what name did you register under?"

Victoria sputtered and laughed. "Oh, you. Oh, Charity. You are too much."

"Tell me."

"No, you tell me. What name did you register at school under?"

"Cari. Caridad."

"Ah. *Sí. Bien.*"

"But you, once you leave RDS, you are no longer Victoria. Therefore, you are . . . who?"

She shrugged, then finally answered, "Linda."

"Really?"

"Yes. Linda Valdes."

"That's your name?"

"Yes. What do you think?"

"I love it. It's a good professional name. A lawyer's name."

"You think so?"

"I do. Yes. Maybe I will pay a professional call on you someday."

Victoria laughed. "I would like that." Then she added seriously, "But for two more weeks, until my notice is up, I will remain Victoria. That's what my contract stipulates."

"Stipulates? That sounds very professional."

"Yes. It does. And it's the right thing to do, you know? It's what Ramiro Fortunato would do."

I answered like Dessi. "But Ramiro Fortunato is a character. He isn't real."

Victoria feigned shock. "Don't say that. He is a hero!"

I leaned in front of her so she'd have to look me in the eye.
"He never sat up all night next to a child, as her protector, and
then worked all the next day for that child, as her maid.
Without sleep. Every night. Every day. For three years."

"No. It wasn't three years."

"It was almost three years."

"Well, then, say 'almost.' Don't exaggerate."

"No one would have done that for me but you."

Victoria held up a finger and pointed it at me. "Yes.
Someone else would have done that. Your mother."

"Really? You think she would have?"

"I know it. And I know that you will do that, too, for your
child."

I thought about her words, and I chose my own words
carefully. "Well, maybe I would have grown up to be like her,
like my mother, but I didn't get the chance." I looked into
Victoria's black eyes with my brown ones. "Instead, I grew up
to be like you."

We stayed in that moment for a long time. Then, out of
the corner of my eye, I saw my father walking over with his
old-man gait, and I knew I had to go. I leaned forward, kissed
her lightly on the cheek, and managed to say *"Adiós."*

She whispered, "Don't become like that old man over
there. Don't forget to live your life. Don't miss out on the adventure, on the thrill of it all."

"I won't. *Te amo, Victoria. Te amo, Linda.*"

"Te amo, Cari." She kissed me back, turned me by my shoulders, and gave me a soft push, sending me toward my father on a pair of unsteady legs.

One look at my face told him not to say a word. Instead, he took my arm and started to lead me away, slowly and silently, through the raucous crowd. I twisted my head around occasionally to look back, but I kept my legs moving straight ahead, straight toward our car and our new life down south.

I caught sight of Mickie and Dessi, still standing on the stage. I saw the Highlands kids, still hiding behind their guards. Soon, however, all those people from my past life were only tiny figures in the distance, no bigger than *tornadas*.

When we arrived at La Iglesia de la Natividad, my father paused for a moment to rest. I stood and admired the outdoor crèche. It was a rough, wood-carved barn packed full of delicate characters—angels, shepherds, kings, a baby Jesus. It was a beautiful sight.

I'd have admired it longer, but a gang of revelers, laughing and singing, ran up and squirted us with water. I jumped in fright, and then I laughed. I shook the cold water out of my hair and turned to face them. I wished I had my own pistol to squirt them back, but when I looked at my father, he was clearly not up to a challenge. His face showed nothing but weariness and impatience and worry. He took my arm again and, with a disapproving look at the revelers, moved us along.

I followed my father's lead past food booths and game stands and clothing stalls. He did not pause at any of them. He led us on an inexorable march (a Mrs. Veck word) back toward our parking space. Just as we reached the red-and-white banner, though, I pulled my arm away and forced him to stop. I turned around, stood tall in my clogs, and scanned the stage area, trying to spot Victoria.

And there she was! A tiny figure, still standing by the oak tree. She was watching me. I waved to her but, to my surprise, she did not wave back. Not exactly. Instead, she raised her arm and pointed energetically to her right, and then her left, and then in front. She kept pointing at things until I understood what she meant: she was pointing at *everything*. Everything around us. She was telling me to open my eyes, damn it, and see it all. To become part of it all.

I gave my father a sideways glance. He had his car keys out, and he was fingering them nervously. I took one step forward. I looked him full in the face, shook my head, and mouthed the word "no."

He asked, "*¿Qué, Cari?* What is it? Can we go?"

"No. We cannot. I am not ready to leave."

I watched his lips rub together under his white mustache. He whispered, "But our work . . ."

"Our work can wait for just a few hours. Can't it, Papi?"

He seemed genuinely surprised by the question. "*¿Por qué?*"

"*Por* living life."

"Living life?"

"*Sí.*"

He thought for a moment—very, very hard—and then he started to change before my eyes. Suddenly all the impatience and worry seemed to pass from his face like a swift cloud. His brow lost its wrinkles; his back lost its hunch. He answered me, with true contrition, "*Sí, Cari.* Of course. Of course it can. I am sorry. I am so sorry."

"Then we can stay?"

"Yes. We *must* stay. We must stay and do some living. Forgive me, please."

I told him, "I forgive you," and I stared at him until he managed a sheepish smile. I walked behind him and gently turned his shoulders until he was facing the distant stage. Then I leaned closer and shouted in his ear, *"Ahora! Atención, Papi!"* His head snapped up and his eyes snapped open wider. I left him standing there at attention, positively beaming, like a silly wooden soldier.

Now my own time had come.

I drew a deep breath, straightened my corte, and finger-combed my hair. I walked quickly back toward La Iglesia de la Natividad, stopping at the first booth I saw to purchase a plastic water gun. I negotiated the sale in perfect Spanish, thinking about that gang of water squirters with vengeance on my mind.

Once I was armed and loaded, I plunged back into the sea of colorful costumes, swirling dancers, and pulsing rhythms. Then, for the rest of that bright and sunny afternoon, under the watchful eyes of my father at one end and Victoria at the other, I started living my new life. Slowly at first, but then with mounting confidence, I let myself be swept away by the fun and the adventure and the exitement—by the wondrous thrill of it all.